# THE
# MIDNIGHT
# MYSTERY

Other books by
BETTY REN WRIGHT

# THE MIDNIGHT MYSTERY

Original title: *Rosie and the Dance of the Dinosaurs*

## Betty Ren Wright

AN
**APPLE**
PAPERBACK

SCHOLASTIC INC.
New York Toronto London Auckland Sydney

ISBN 0-590-43758-5

Copyright © 1989 by Betty Ren Wright. All rights reserved. Published by Scholastic Inc., 730 Broadway, New York, NY 10003, by arrangement with Holiday House, Inc. APPLE PAPERBACKS is a registered trademark of Scholastic Inc.

12 11 10 9 8 7 6 5 4                                        2 3 4 5 6/9

Printed in the U.S.A.                                        40

First Scholastic printing, July 1991

*For my mother,*
REN WRIGHT,
*who was in the front row,*
*and cheering, at every*
*recital.*

# THE MIDNIGHT MYSTERY

# CHAPTER 1

Rosie heard the sound under her couch-bed almost as soon as she slid between the sheets. It was below her feet, a tiny skittering sound that could have been a mouse. She lay very still and tried not to hear. If she mentioned the sound, her mother, sitting in a rocking chair at the other end of the screened-in porch, would be frightened. Everything scared Mama these days. Mice. Sudden noises. Leaky faucets. Everything.

"Can't you sleep, Rosie? Does the lamp bother you? I'll go inside to read if the light keeps you awake."

"No problem," Rosie mumbled. It was what her father used to say. No problem to fix the drip in the bathtub. No problem to tighten the knobs on the drawers of her desk. No problem, no problem, right up to the day, a month ago, when he'd moved to Milwaukee.

Rosie's mother sighed.

The sound came again. Skitter. Skitter. *Swiiish*. Something with claws under the couch, trying to get out. Rosie snuggled into the sheets and clutched Bert Bear. Now she wished Mama *would* hear the noise. She wished, even more, that her father were sitting in the other rocking chair, reading *Fishing Facts* and drinking lemonade.

"What's that?" Mama looked up sharply. "Did you hear a noise, Rosie? I believe there's a *mouse* under the couch."

Rosie closed her eyes. Mama sounded terrified, but surely she'd have to do something about the noise, now that she'd heard it. The rocker creaked, and tip-toeing steps crossed to the kitchen. The screen door flip-flopped softly, and Rosie and Bert Bear were alone on the porch.

Skitter. *Swiiish*.

The door flip-flopped again. Rosie opened her eyes a crack, enough to see the broom her mother was carrying.

"Don't be afraid," Mama said in a trembling voice. "It's just a *mouse,* dear."

Rosie pulled the sheet over her head and hugged Bert tighter than ever. The broom brushed across the floor under the couch. It started at one end, under Rosie's head, and swooshed to her feet. Then Mama screamed—a terrible scream that curled Rosie's toes and frizzled her eyebrows.

"It's a *bat!*" Mama shrieked. "No, no, no!" There was a clatter of footsteps across the porch, and this time the door to the kitchen closed with a slap.

"Rosie," Mama cried from inside the house. "Sweetheart! Stay under the sheet. It's a bat. He's shooting around the porch like a crazy thing. I don't know what to do."

Rosie lay as straight and stiff as a mummy in a museum. She pressed her nose and toes against the sheet. Bert's arm was hard under her ribs, but she didn't dare move.

She tried to remember what she knew about bats. They didn't hurt people, unless they were sick with rabies. They didn't bump into things in the dark. They ate bugs. A bat was about the size of a mouse with wings, and it looked scary even if it wasn't.

Rosie shuddered.

"Sweetheart, are you all right?" Mama sounded as if she were crying. "Will you be okay while I go next door and get Mr. Larsen? He'll know what to—oh, nooooo!" The sentence ended in a wail.

Rosie felt a feather-light touch on her toes. She pulled the sheet tighter over her head and looked down. Through the tent the sheet made she could see a dark shadow. The bat had landed close to her feet and was creeping toward her head.

From where she was under the sheet, he didn't look like a mouse with wings. He looked as big as an eagle.

"No, noooo!" Mama wailed again from the kitchen, her voice rising and falling like the siren of a fire truck.

Rosie watched the shadow moving up the sheet. People could die of fright, couldn't they? If it reached her face, she thought she would die. She considered bouncing the sheet up and down to throw the bat off, but she was too frightened to try it. Bouncing might make him angry, and an angry bat might be meaner than one that was just taking a walk on a sheet.

The shadow reached her middle, denting the sheet ever so slightly as it moved. "Ma-ma!" Rosie bawled. "Help me!"

The screen door burst open and her mother flew out onto the porch as if a great hand had shoved her. *Swoosh*—the broom swept across the sheet, missing the bat shadow completely. *Swoosh*—it swept again. The bat disappeared.

"Go—go, go!" Mama wailed, the siren sound changing now. "Oh, I did it, Rosie, I did it! He's gone!"

Rosie sat up. She gulped in big swallows of sweet night air and looked at her mother in amazement. Mama was standing at the open back door, her face flushed, her long dark hair free of its combs. The broom rested on her shoulder like a hunter's rifle, and she stared out into the darkness of the backyard.

"Where'd it go?" Rosie asked.

"I just opened the door and swept it out." Mama

closed the door and showed how she'd used the broom. "I didn't think about it—I just did it! I can hardly believe I had the nerve." She plunked into the rocking chair and propped the broom between her knees.

"What if he flew the other way?" Rosie wondered. It was okay to play what-if, after the danger was past. "What if he had flown right at you instead of going out the door? What would you have done then?"

Her mother leaned back and closed her eyes. The porch was quiet except for the slow creak of the rocker. "I don't know," Mama said, "I just don't know." Something—Rosie's question or a painful thought—had washed away the excitement in her voice and left a sad little whisper. "I can't forgive your father for being way off in Milwaukee at a moment like this," she said softly. "It makes me want to cry just thinking about it."

"He can't help it," Rosie said. She settled back on her pillow. After all, it wasn't Papa's fault that the insurance company he worked for made him transfer to their Milwaukee office. The iron mines around Dexter were closing, and people weren't buying insurance. Business would pick up again someday, Papa had assured her. *But meanwhile,* he'd added, *I'm going to Milwaukee. We have to eat.*

"If the bat had flown straight at you, you could have thrown a pillow at him," Rosie suggested to make Mama feel better. "Or you could have done a magic spell. You could have said, 'Bat, bat, here's your hat. Now you'd better scat, scat, scat.'"

Her mother started to smile. "If you're so smart," Mama said, "why did you call for help, Miss Know-It-All? Why didn't you say the magic spell and get rid of him yourself?"

"I wanted to," Rosie said, "but Bert kept poking me and poking me, till I couldn't remember the words. Bears are awfully afraid of bats."

"Well, at least they admit it," Mama said. She reached up and turned off the lamp, letting soft dark settle around them. "Go to sleep now, Rosie, it's getting late."

"Bert can't sleep," Rosie said, after a minute, "he's still too scared." She knew she was too old for stuffed animals, but Bert had been her friend for as long as she could remember. She and Mama and Papa all treated him like one of the family.

Mama came over to the edge of the couch. She patted Bert's brown head, squeezed his ears gently, and hummed "Red River Valley" in her shaky, off-key voice.

It must have been the ear-squeezing that did it. Bert was asleep in two minutes, a bear grin on his nice old face. Rosie watched him for a while, and then she closed her eyes.

"Don't go away," she said, "in case the bat comes back." That sounded babyish, too, but she didn't care.

"He won't be back," Mama whispered. "He's out in the yard playing Super-Bat with his brothers and sisters. But I'll stay anyway."

# CHAPTER 2

Rosie was practicing her recital piece the next morning when an old truck pulled into the driveway. There was a box standing upright in the back of the truck. It was made of shiny wood and was as tall as a telephone booth. The doors had copper-colored knobs.

Rosie stopped playing "The Dance of the Dinosaurs" and ran out on the back porch. "What is it?" she asked Mama.

Two men lifted the box out of the truck and carried it up the back steps. Rosie's mother held the door open and then hurried ahead to hold the kitchen door, too. "Take it right upstairs, please," she said. "It goes in the first room on the right. The far corner."

"That's my room," Rosie protested. "What *is* it?"

"A surprise," her mother said happily. "I found it at a garage sale. All these years you haven't had a closet in your room, but now you have one. No more clothes hanging on pegs all over the walls."

They followed the men upstairs to Rosie's bedroom. The box stood in the corner, with Rosie's desk pushed aside to make space. It looked like an extrawide coffin.

"Papa says I don't need a closet. He says my room looks fine the way it is." Rosie almost added that she liked it better the old way, but then she saw her mother's face cloud with disappointment. "What do you call that box?" she asked.

The disappointed look faded. "You call it a wardrobe," Mama said. "You're going to be glad you have it, dear. Wait and see." She went downstairs with the men, while Rosie sat on the edge of the bed and stared at the wardrobe.

It did look like a coffin. She shivered, remembering now that a wardrobe had been the subject of an argument between her mother and father, only then Rosie hadn't known what a wardrobe was. "She doesn't need one," her father had said, "not at her age. She needs the space more. Why fill up the room with furniture? And besides," he'd added, "why spend money when we may be moving before long?"

Heavy footsteps sounded on the stairs, and the younger of the two men came back into Rosie's room. He was tall, with a sand-colored mustache as wide as a clothes brush. His face was thin and freckled, and he had long ears and bushy eyebrows. He carried two wooden rods.

"Your ma had me fix this up so it's just right for you," he said. He smiled at Rosie as he opened the wardrobe doors. "I'll show you." He motioned Rosie to come closer. "Now, you hold one end of this rod right here, and I'll slide the other end into place."

Rosie saw that fresh holes had been drilled inside the wardrobe so that the two rods fitted snugly, one about three feet above the other. "This low one can hold the stuff you use every day," the man explained. "And you can put your mink jacket and other winter stuff up at the top."

"Who has a mink jacket?" Rosie said. She knew he was teasing her, but she didn't care. She held the rod tightly since the man had asked for help.

"Well, anyway, this'll be real nice for you," he said. "My pa used it for eighty-some years."

"Why doesn't he use it now?" Rosie asked.

"He died last month. We're cleaning out his room and selling a few things. I hate to see his stuff go, but money's a little tight right now. . . ." He broke off suddenly. "Hey, kid, what's wrong with your hand?"

Rosie let go of the rod and curled her right hand into a fist. "Nothing," she snapped. "Nothing's wrong with it." She stopped feeling sorry for the man.

"Sure there is. You've got a finger missing, right? Nothing to be ashamed of—how'd you lose it?"

She decided his mustache looked silly, and she didn't care if he was lonesome for his father and was poor besides. "I didn't *lose* it," she said coldly, "I've always had nine fingers. Nine are all I need." It was what her father had told her to say to anyone rude enough to ask.

The man's freckled face turned red. "Oh, sure," he said. He snapped the second clothes rod in place and shut the wardrobe doors.

"There," he said, "it's all set for your fancy dresses. And there's a nice big drawer down below for your shoes or whatever."

"I don't have any fancy dresses," Rosie said. "I hate fancy dresses." She glared at his mustache. "I'm the best artist in my class," she told him. "Nine fingers are all I need. I make the best clay pots, too."

"Bet you do, at that," the man muttered. He hurried out of the bedroom and thumped down the stairs.

Rosie went out into the hall. "I play the piano," she called after him. "Nine fingers can do anything."

He didn't answer. When she heard the porch door slam and the truck start up at the side of the house, she went back to her bedroom.

*What a dummy!* she thought. But then her anger and hurt feelings began to slip away. The man shouldn't have asked about her hand, but now that he was gone she didn't hate him so much. He hadn't meant to make her feel bad. She hated other people more—the ones who stared and stared at her hand without saying anything at all. She could do everything she wanted to do with nine fingers, until someone stared. Then, not always but once in a while, her fingers stumbled over each other, forgetting what they were able to do.

She scowled at the wardrobe. Then she looked at her fuzzy blue bathrobe hanging from its peg on the wall, her favorite pink-and-white-striped dress, her blue denim skirt safety-pinned to its hanger, her khaki blouse. They were like old friends hanging there. They wouldn't like being hidden away inside the wardrobe. Inside the coffin!

She snatched up Bert Bear and squeezed him so hard that he squealed.

"What are you so angry about?" he seemed to say, when he got his breath back. "It's just a big box, kiddo."

She squeezed him again, gently this time—once because she was sorry she'd been rough, and once because Bert was such a good friend. He loved her all the time, even now, when she felt mean as a snake.

# CHAPTER 3

There was an ugly squawking sound, then Rosie woke up. Her throat ached, and she realized she had made the sound herself. She'd been trying to scream.

Mama rushed into the bedroom and sat on the edge of the bed. "It was just a bad dream, hon," she said. "Calm down now."

"It wasn't *just* a dream," Rosie protested. "It was the worst nightmare in the whole world." She peeked over her mother's shoulder at the wardrobe in the corner.

"The old man was in there," she explained shakily, "in the wardrobe. He was trying to get out, and I was holding the door shut."

Mama looked at the wardrobe, too. "What old man?"

"The dead old man. The one the wardrobe used to

14

belong to. He was angry because his son sold it to us."

Rosie's mother went over and threw open the doors of the wardrobe. The pink-and-white-striped dress hung there, and the khaki blouse, like small ghosts in the dark.

"So." Mama pretended to peer deep into the wardrobe. "Where is that old man? Where can he be? I don't see him anywhere." She closed the door and came back to the bed. "I know what this is all about," she said firmly. "You're upset because you miss your father. Children often have nightmares when they are worried or unhappy about something. Your father has a lot to answer for."

Rosie didn't see how the nightmare could be her father's fault. He didn't even know about the wardrobe. But she didn't want to argue, either. It was easier to lie quietly and wait for the scared feelings to fade.

"Well, it's my opinion that your father will move back here one of these days," Mama said. "He's going to hate living in a big city. You'll see. He'll decide that his job isn't worth leaving Dexter for, and he'll come back to us."

"We could go to Milwaukee and be with him," Rosie whispered.

Mama stood up and smoothed Rosie's hair. "Now don't *you* start," she said. "This is our home, right here in Dexter. In this nice old house where I grew up. Not in some nasty city."

Rosie sighed. She'd heard these words a hundred times, usually late at night when Mama and Papa thought she was sleeping. Mostly, she'd been on her mother's side. She didn't want to leave their house with its pointy roof and blue shutters. She didn't want to leave her best friend Angela Carillo or her school or Mrs. Kramer, her piano teacher.

But if there were no jobs in Dexter...

"Let me know when you're ready to come," her father had said that last, terrible day. "I'll have a nice place waiting for you." And then he was gone, and she and Mama were alone. Rosie could still hardly believe he had left them. She knew her mother felt the same way.

"Tomorrow night I want to sleep on the back porch again," Rosie said. "I like it out there."

Mama switched off the lamp. "If the weather's warm enough," she promised. "The porch is one of the things I love about this house. One of many things." She went back to her bedroom, and Rosie and Bert Bear were alone with the wardrobe once more.

Bert turned his back to the wardrobe. "We'll get used to it," Rosie whispered. "Tomorrow we'll probably even like it."

She was wrong. In the morning the wardrobe looked as threatening as ever, and Rosie was glad she didn't have to open it to get dressed. Her shorts and shirts were folded in the dresser drawer where they'd always been. One running shoe was under the bed, and the other was under the desk. She dressed in a hurry, dragged a comb through her hair, and hurried downstairs.

"I'm not hungry," she told her mother. "I have to practice."

Her mother looked up from the newspaper. "Breakfast first," she said. "You mustn't do all your practicing the day before your lesson, Rosie."

"I've practiced every day."

"Ten minutes here, ten minutes there. It'll take more than that to be ready for the recital. Barely three weeks to go, you know."

Rosie felt a familiar clutch in her tummy. Three weeks—she'd been thinking about that while she dressed, and it was the reason why she didn't feel like eating. "The Dance of the Dinosaurs" was the hardest piece she'd ever played. Even with the special fingering Mrs. Kramer had worked out—for nine fingers instead of ten—it was hard.

"What if I can't play in the recital?" Rosie said, pouring a little bit of cereal into her bowl. "What if I'm sick?"

"If you are, you'll get better in a hurry," Mama said. "A miracle recovery—I'll see to it."

They were still at the table when Angela tapped at the porch door and let herself in. Her black hair was brushed back and held in place with pink clips with roses on them. Her eyes shone with important news.

"We're going to see my cousin," she said. "They're

all settled in their new house, and we're invited to see it."

Rosie put down her spoon. "Your cousin Mary Jean Weiss?"

Angela nodded. "You can come along if you want to. My mom said so."

"Rosie should practice her piano lesson," Mama said.

Rosie was relieved. She wanted to see Mary Jean's house, and yet she didn't.

Ever since the Weisses came to Dexter from Chicago months ago, Angela had been talking about Mary Jean. She was beautiful, and she was going to have a swimming pool and a puppy when they moved into their new house. At first it had been fun, like hearing about a fairy princess, but then Mary Jean had started piano lessons with Mrs. Kramer. All of a sudden, she was *real*. She came for her lesson right after Rosie, and she was as pretty as Angela had claimed. Once or twice Rosie had lingered in the front yard to hear Mary Jean play. She sounded like a pianist, not a little girl taking her lesson. Angela said she'd been studying piano in Chicago for a long time.

"We'll be back before lunch," Angela said. "You'll have this afternoon to practice, Rosie."

"Well, that's all right, I guess," Mama said. And just like that it was settled, without anyone asking Rosie if she wanted to go.

"How's your recital piece coming, Angela?" Mama asked. "Are you going to be ready?"

Angela wrinkled her nose, rolled her eyes, and tugged the lobes of her ears before she answered. "I'll never be ready, Mrs. Carpenter," she said. "I'll forget, or I'll skip a page, or something. I don't care. I'd rather roller-skate, anyway. That's what I want to be—a champion roller-skater."

"You mustn't say you don't care," Rosie's mother scolded. "You want to make your family proud of you."

Angela helped herself to an apple from the bowl in the middle of the table. "They can be proud of Mary Jean," she said. "Mary Jean's going to be the last player on the program. That means she's the star of the recital."

Rosie and Mama looked at each other. "How do you know she's going to play last?" Mama asked.

"Mrs. Kramer told Aunt Marcia—that's Mary Jean's mom—and Aunt Marcia told my mom. Mary Jean is a prodigy."

"What's a prodigy?" Rosie tried to sound as if she wasn't really interested.

"It's a young person who does especially well at something," Mama explained. "Did Mrs. Kramer actually say Mary Jean is a prodigy?"

Angela shrugged. "Aunt Marcia said it. Maybe Mrs. Kramer said it first. Aunt Marcia says Mary Jean is a born musician."

"Rosie has something new up in her room to show you," Mama said, changing the subject. "It's something very nice. Take Angela upstairs, hon."

With dragging feet, Rosie led the way to the stairs. She felt lower than a grasshopper's knees. For months—ever since Mrs. Kramer had given her the music for "The Dance of the Dinosaurs"—she had dreamed of being the last player in the recital. Last meant best. Now Mrs. Kramer had chosen Mary Jean instead—Mary Jean, the prodigy.

Going up the stairs, Rosie stuffed her right hand into the pocket of her jeans. That was that, she thought. Mrs. Kramer didn't think she could possibly play well enough to be the star. She didn't believe nine fingers would be enough.

At the top of the stairs, Angela ran ahead and peeked into the bedroom. Her eyes widened.

"There's a coffin in there," she squealed. "A double coffin. Hey, what's inside of it, Rosie? Two mummies wrapped up in sheets? Or two vampires? I hope it's vampires. I love vampires!"

"It's not a coffin, it's a wardrobe," Rosie said crossly. "In place of a closet." She opened the big doors to show her clothes hanging in a row. "Mama bought it for me. It's old."

Angela didn't say anything, but Rosie knew what her friend was thinking. She wouldn't want a double coffin in the corner of *her* bedroom.

"Well, what do you think of Rosie's wardrobe?" Mama asked when they returned to the kitchen. "Pretty nice, huh?"

Angela hesitated. "I guess so, Mrs. Carpenter. Only it looks sort of like a—"

"I forgot to tell you about the bat," Rosie interrupted. "Wait'll you hear what happened." She began her story fast, before Angela could tell Mama what the wardrobe looked like.

When she described how Mama had swept the bat into the backyard, Angela giggled. "You're really brave, Mrs. Carpenter," she said. *"My* mother wouldn't have done that. She would have screamed her head off till my father came. That's how it is at our house."

"If I screamed my head off, I'd just have to pick it up and put it back on," Mama said. "That's how it is at *our* house." She smiled, but her eyes looked shiny.

Angela shifted from one foot to the other. "We'd better go," she said. "My mom'll be waiting for us."

Rosie gave her mother a hug and followed Angela out the back door. She still wasn't sure she wanted to go to Mary Jean's new house, but she didn't feel like practicing "The Dance of the Dinosaurs" either. She didn't even want to play in the stupid recital anymore.

There was only one person who could possibly make her feel better, and he was hundreds of miles away in Milwaukee. *What's the difference whether you're first, last, or in the middle?* he'd say. *You're the best, cookie!* And she'd have to cheer up a little, even though he only said it because he loved her.

# CHAPTER 4

Rosie knew Mary Jean's house was going to be special, because even though it was new, it had tall trees all around it. Most new houses had little stick-trees in their front yards, but Mary Jean's stood in a circle of shade.

"The swimming pool's in back," Angela reported as she and her mother and Rosie trooped up to the front door. "And there's all kinds of playground stuff for Eldon—that's Mary Jean's little brother. There's a puppy, too. He chews things."

"I'd rather have ten naughty puppies than one Eldon," Mrs. Carillo said unexpectedly. She raised her eyebrows at Rosie as she thumped the big brass knocker.

The door opened and they stepped into a cool, bright entrance hall. "Welcome, welcome," Mrs.

Weiss chanted in a breathy little-girl voice. Slim with yellow-gold hair, she might have been Mary Jean's older sister.

She led them proudly through the downstairs rooms. Angela and her mother had been there several times before, but this was the first time all the furniture was in place and all the appliances worked.

"I'm glad you came, too, Rosie," Mrs. Weiss said. "Mary Jean must make some friends here in Dexter. Of course, once school starts this fall, she'll know everybody."

"Where *is* Mary Jean?" Angela asked after they had admired the draperies in the living room and Mrs. Carillo had warned the girls to check the bottoms of their shoes before walking across the creamy carpet.

Mrs. Weiss pointed toward the stairway that seemed to float up from the middle of the entrance hall. "She's in her room—listen."

Piano music, light as a summer breeze, drifted down the stairs.

"She's been practicing for an hour," Mrs. Weiss said proudly. "The recital, you know. You girls can go right up if you want to."

Rosie followed Angela across the thick carpet and up the stairs. The music grew louder.

"How can she practice up here?" Rosie whispered when they reached the second-floor hallway. "The piano's downstairs."

Angela grinned and pointed into the nearest room. "Look."

Rosie looked. Across an expanse of blue, Mary Jean sat at a small white piano. A white piano—in her bedroom! Rosie could hardly believe it. She might have imagined the bed with its lacy canopy and the ruffled dressing table, even the huge dollhouse—but a white piano? Never! This bedroom was perfect.

"Hey, Mary Jean," Angela said, "you hit a sour note."

Rosie gasped, and Mary Jean stopped playing and turned around with a little frown. "I did not," she snapped. Then she saw Rosie. "You take lessons from Mrs. Kramer, too," she said. "Hi."

Rosie pushed her right hand deep into her pocket. It was what she always did when she met someone new.

"This is Rosie Carpenter," Angela announced. "This is my cousin Mary Jean. May I show her the dollhouse?"

"I'll show her," Mary Jean said. She slid off the white piano bench. "My mother had it made for me. In New York."

Rosie stood in front of the dollhouse for a long time. She loved it all, but she couldn't stop looking in the attic. It held a tiny trunk with a padlock no bigger than the head of a match. There was an old-fashioned cradle and a straight-backed chair and a stack of little flowered hatboxes. Best of all was the window seat tucked into a gable. A book was open on the window seat, and next to it lay a tiny plastic apple. The gable was someone's favorite reading-corner, just as it would be Rosie's if she lived in the dollhouse.

She studied the blue bedroom and the rose one, the bathroom with its stack of neatly folded blue-and-white towels, the dining room, ready for a party, and the living room full of fragile chairs and postage-stamp-sized paintings.

"It's beautiful," Rosie breathed. Almost without knowing it, she reached out her left hand to pick up a gold-and-crystal lamp on one of the tables. Mary Jean's cool voice stopped her before she touched it. "I don't *play* with it," she said. "Everything breaks."

There was a thud behind them, and a rubber ball rolled across the carpet. A little boy, no more than four or five, peeked around the doorway. When he saw the girls' startled faces, he stuck out his tongue.

"Go away!" Mary Jean shrieked. She dashed across the room, but he was already gone, making hooting sounds as he raced down the hall. Mary Jean slammed the door. Her face was pink with anger.

"He's the worst kid in the whole world," she muttered. "I call him Eldon the Horrible."

Rosie started to say she'd always wanted a little brother, but then she remembered Mrs. Carillo's comment. *I'd rather have ten naughty puppies than one Eldon.* Still, throwing a ball and sticking out his tongue didn't seem such horrible things to do.

The girls admired the dollhouse awhile longer, and then Mary Jean showed them the rest of her bedroom —the dressing table, the big closet with built-in drawers and shelves (so different from a wardrobe), the pink-and-white bathroom with its pink soap and pink bubble bath.

"Girls," Mary Jean's mother called from the foot of the stairs, "how about some lemonade and cookies?"

"Let's go," Angela said. She'd seen most of Mary Jean's room before and was getting bored.

With a last, loving look at the dollhouse, Rosie followed the others downstairs and out onto the patio at the back of the house. Mrs. Carillo was already there, sitting next to the empty pool.

"Next week it'll be finished and they'll put in the water," Mary Jean said. "Then we can swim."

Rosie's heart jumped at the word "we." Did Mary Jean mean they were going to be friends, and Rosie would be invited to this house again? Or did the "we" mean Mary Jean and Eldon and their parents? Rosie was wondering how to find out, when there was a cry from inside the house.

"Oh, no!" It was Mrs. Weiss's voice raised in a wail.

They dashed through the dining room to the big copper-and-white kitchen. Mrs. Weiss was at the counter staring at the blender. A cookie jar stood close at hand.

"What in the world is wrong, Marcia?" Mrs. Carillo demanded. "You sound as if you've seen a ghost."

*Or a bat,* Rosie said under her breath. Her own mother had wailed just like that.

Mrs. Weiss pointed at the cookie jar. It was filled nearly to the top with crumbs. Funny crumbs, Rosie thought, colored with spatters of red and blue and green.

"Cookies," Mrs. Weiss gasped. "Eldon...I spent hours...colored frosting...." She took a deep breath. "Eldon has been very naughty," she said shakily. "Now I don't have any cookies to serve you."

"You mean Eldon ground them all up, Aunt Marcia?" Angela's brown eyes popped. "Wow!"

"Oh, for heaven's sake!" Mrs. Carillo shook her head. "I'd wallop that child!"

Mrs. Weiss looked shocked. "I'm sure it's my fault," she said. "He wanted to play with the blender, and I wouldn't let him. Then I went outside to work in the garden, and Mary Jean was practicing and... well, we just shouldn't have left him alone."

Rosie wondered what her own mother would do at a time like this. One thing was certain: She wouldn't tell people it was *her* fault that Rosie had been naughty. There would be a lot of scolding and at least a week of no desserts. Rosie had a feeling that neither of these things would happen to Eldon.

As if to prove she was right, Mrs. Weiss gestured toward a tray that held tall glasses of lemonade. "We might as well take those out to the patio," she said. "Mary Jean, run upstairs and tell your brother we're having our lemonade now."

Mary Jean stuck out her lip. "I hate him!" she exclaimed. "I won't tell him anything."

"He's just a *little* boy," her mother said. "We must remember that."

Mrs. Carillo tightened her lips as if she wanted to say something but thought she'd better not. Mary Jean stamped out of the kitchen, heading toward the patio. "I don't want any old lemonade," she muttered. "Lemonade is boring without cookies."

Mrs. Weiss sighed and picked up the tray. "Well, the rest of us can have a cool drink anyway," she said. "Angela, would you mind running upstairs to see if you can find Eldon? He does love lemonade, and besides—"

"Besides, he could be getting into trouble again," Angela said. "Come on, Rosie."

Rosie was glad to go; she might have a chance to look at the dollhouse once more. The girls hurried upstairs, hesitating at Mary Jean's bedroom door.

"I hear splashing in the bathroom," Rosie said.

They tiptoed across the carpet and stood outside the bathroom door looking at each other. Finally, Angela eased the door open a crack.

Rosie guessed what was happening even before she leaned forward and peeked through the opening. The smell of lilac filled the air. Eldon was in the bathtub, covered to his round little chin with pink bubbles that overflowed the tub and sailed into the steamy air. He grinned at the girls and tossed a handful of bubbles at them.

Angela slammed the door. "The whole bottle," she

gasped. "He must have poured the whole bottle of bubble bath into the tub."

Rosie nodded. She'd caught a glimpse of the bubble-bath bottle lying on the rug.

"You go down and tell Aunt Marcia," Angela said. "I'll guard the door in case he decides to run all over the house trailing bubbles."

Rosie shook her head. It would be bad enough telling Mrs. Weiss, but she hated to think of what Mary Jean might do when she heard what was happening in her private bathroom. She'd probably race upstairs and try to drown Eldon.

"You go," she said. "I'll stay here and guard."

In the end they both went. Angela whispered the news to her mother, and Mrs. Carillo repeated it, as calmly as possible, to Mrs. Weiss. Mrs. Weiss leaned back in her canvas chair and closed her eyes.

Mary Jean had been sitting on the edge of the empty pool. She heard one word, and it was enough to make her scramble to her feet. "Bubbles?" she roared. "What did you say about bubbles?" She raced into the house. "I'll kill him!" she howled. "Just wait till I get my hands on him!"

Mrs. Carillo stood up. "Marcia, you have enough to handle here without having guests, too," she said firmly. "The girls and I will run along while you go upstairs—"

Mrs. Weiss looked as if upstairs was the last place where she wanted to be. "Please don't go," she said in a weak little voice. But Mrs. Carillo raised her eyebrows at Angela and Rosie, and they followed her willingly across the patio.

"We'll be back another day, dear," Mrs. Carillo called. "The house is lovely."

"Thanks for inviting me," Rosie said. "I had fun."

There was a scream from upstairs that sent them running down the front walk to the car.

They were all very quiet on the way home. Finally Angela spoke. "We didn't see the puppy," she said.

"And you won't," her mother replied, tight-lipped. "Aunt Marcia said they had to return him to the breeder. Eldon was teasing him from morning till night."

"I've never met any rich people before," Rosie said. "Mary Jean is lucky."

"They're a very lucky family," Mrs. Carillo said in a funny, dry voice, "though I doubt that they know it. Marcia's father owned half of downtown Dexter, and other property besides. She inherited it all. Nobody has to worry about a job in *that* family."

Angela poked Rosie in the ribs. "Rosie wants a little brother," she said slyly. "Maybe she can have Eldon. Even if he *is* spoiled."

"Both those kids are spoiled rotten," Mrs. Carillo said. "It's a shame. Their father—he's my younger brother, Rosie—he's as helpless as Marcia is. There're worse things than being an only child, and being spoiled rotten is one of 'em."

Rosie nodded. "I don't need a brother," she said. It was true. She didn't need a brother or a dollhouse or a white piano in her bedroom. There was only one thing she really needed that she didn't have.

"My father could make Eldon behave," she said.

Her father could do anything.

# CHAPTER 5

"I'll never be able to do it," Rosie groaned. "My fingers get tangled every time."

Mrs. Kramer looked at Rosie over the tops of her glasses. "Never say never, Rose. Now, start from the top of the page, and try not to tense up. There's no reason why you can't play that run as well as anyone else."

Rosie gritted her teeth. There *was* a reason, and for the first time in her life she was ready to admit it. Nine fingers weren't enough! She knew it, and Mrs. Kramer knew it, too.

The run—eighteen fast notes up and eighteen down—came near the end of "The Dance of the Dinosaurs." It was glittering and beautiful when Mrs. Kramer played it, and until now Rosie had believed she could make it sound beautiful, too, if she practiced hard enough. But ever since Angela had told her Mary Jean was to be last in the recital, things had changed. Now Rosie knew Mrs. Kramer didn't think she could play well enough to be the star. And if Mrs. Kramer had doubts, how could Rosie believe she could do it?

She leaned forward, as if getting closer to the music might help. Her fingers felt thick and clumsy. Her shoulders ached.

"Relax," Mrs. Kramer murmured, "just relax, Rose."

Rosie flattened her hands across the keys. "I can't do it," she said.

There was an uneasy silence.

"I can't," Rosie repeated.

Mrs. Kramer sighed. "We'll let the run go for a bit," she suggested. "How are you doing on the memorizing?"

"Okay," Rosie said. It was a lie.

"Show me," Mrs. Kramer ordered. She closed the sheet music and put it on the table next to the piano.

Rosie curved her fingers over the keyboard and began. Maybe this time—but, no. After the first few bars she stumbled and came to a stop.

"I still get kind of mixed up," she confessed. "I know some of the parts, but I can't put them together. . . ."

Suddenly she was close to tears. Nothing like this had ever happened to her before.

"What is it, Rose?" Mrs. Kramer asked gently.

"Are things going badly at home?" She put an arm around Rosie's shoulders.

"No." Rosie wiggled away. She didn't want to talk about home. "Everything's okay."

"Well, then," Mrs. Kramer said slowly, "I wonder if we should just put aside 'The Dance of the Dinosaurs' and work on something else."

"We can't," Rosie said desperately. "There isn't time. The recital—"

"You can play the same piece you played last year," Mrs. Kramer said. "'Grandpa's Farm,' wasn't it? You did that very well."

*The same piece you played last year!* Rosie stared at her teacher. How could she play the same piece? She was a whole year older. "Grandpa's Farm" was for babies!

"I don't want to play anything but 'The Dance of the Dinosaurs'!" Rosie exclaimed. "I love it!"

"Well, then, you'll just have to work harder, won't you?" Mrs. Kramer said. "You'll have to work very hard on that run—play it slowly for a while—and work very hard on memorizing. Then we'll see."

"See what?" Rosie asked. She was afraid of the answer.

"See how it goes," Mrs. Kramer replied, which could mean anything at all.

On the way home, Rosie kicked a bottle cap from one side of the pavement to the other. Back and forth. Back and forth. It was true, she supposed, that she hadn't been practicing hard enough. But she didn't have her father to cheer her on, and that made a difference. Her mother tried, but it wasn't the same.

It was a relief to turn down her own block and see her old gray house waiting. She'd practice an hour every day, she decided. Maybe it wouldn't change anything, but she'd try.

"Mama!" She stopped just inside the front hall. The house was very quiet. Mama had to be here someplace, reading or sewing or cleaning out a drawer. Any second now, she'd call hello.

The back door slammed. Rosie ran through the house and out onto the porch. The yard was empty.

"Mama? Where are you?" Someone must have slammed that door.

Why didn't her mother answer? Rosie looked beyond the maple tree to the garage, closed up tight, and beyond that to the row of lilac bushes at the end of the yard. She tried to find her mother's figure in the shifting light and shadow, but she wasn't there. No one was there.

Rosie went out to the garage and peered on tiptoe through one of the glass panels in the door. The car wasn't there either.

With dragging steps she went back to the house. This time she noticed the note propped up on the kitchen table against a vase of daisies.

*Gone to the store, hon,* it said. *Be back soon. Set the table.* The time, *4:15,* was scrawled in the corner.

Rosie felt a chill, like a cold finger on the back of

her neck. It was 4:30 now. Her mother had left fifteen minutes ago, and yet Rosie had just heard the back door slam. Someone had been in the house and had run away when Rosie called.

The telephone rang on the counter close to her elbow. She snatched it up and said "Hello," in a voice that didn't sound like her own.

"Hey, Rosie, is that you?"

*"Papa!"* How had he known she was alone and frightened?

"You okay, kiddo? You sound funny."

"Yes. . . . I don't know. . . . When are you coming home?"

There was a silence while Rosie gripped the phone hard. The question had popped out because she needed him so much. After a moment, she realized he wasn't going to answer it.

"Is your mama there, kiddo? I told her I'd call about five today, but I got through work early."

"She's at the grocery store."

"You're there alone?"

"I just got home from my piano lesson." She wanted to tell him about the slamming back door, but if she did, he'd tell her to go next door to the Larsens' right away. She didn't want him to hang up. As long as he was there at the end of the line, she wasn't afraid of anything.

"How's it going—the piano lessons? You all set for the big recital?"

"No." The word came out more sharply than Rosie

intended. Quickly, she told him about the difficult run in the final section of "The Dance of the Dinosaurs," and how hard it was to memorize the music. "I can't do it," she wailed. "I can't! And Mrs. Kramer says maybe I'll have to play last year's piece."

"That's crazy," her father said. "You *can* do it, Rosie. If the run's hard, you'll just have to play it a few hundred times till it feels right."

Rosie sniffed. A few hundred times!

"Nine fingers—" she began, but her father cut her short.

"That has nothing to do with it, kiddo," he said sternly. "Nine fingers don't make any difference. Deciding you can do it will make the difference."

When Rosie didn't say anything, he hurried on. "Listen, I have an idea to help with the memorizing. How about this? You make up a story to fit the music —a story about dinosaurs. Then you tell it to yourself while you're playing, and that'll help you remember what part comes next. What do you think?"

Rosie scowled into the telephone. She wanted to tell her father that nothing would help as much as having him move back home, but she knew hearing it would make him unhappy. Besides, he must know how much she missed him. She shouldn't have to tell him.

"You try that, kiddo. Okay?"

"Okay."

"You still sound funny," her father said. "What's wrong—besides the recital piece, I mean?"

Rosie hesitated. "I think there was someone in the house when I came home," she said. "I heard the back door slam."

"What?" Suddenly he was shouting. "Rosie, go outside at once! No, go next door and stay with the Larsens till your mother gets home. Do you hear me? Whoever it was might still be hanging around."

"I don't think—" Rosie began, but he didn't let her finish.

"Go now! GO!"

Rosie hung up the phone and went outside. In some ways, a phone call was worse than not hearing at all, she decided. Her father's voice filled her ears, but she couldn't feel his arms around her keeping her safe. He could *tell* her she'd be able to play "The Dance of the Dinosaurs," but he couldn't make her believe it was true.

She was about to knock on the Larsens' screen door when Mama drove into the yard and waved to her.

# CHAPTER 6

Thunder grumbled in the distance, the sound of a dinosaur waking up. Rosie's house was asleep; she could feel its sleepiness all around her, even though she was wide awake herself.

She kept thinking about her father's telephone calls. The first one had left her feeling sad. The second one, an hour after she and Mama and Mr. Larsen had searched the house from attic to basement, was much more cheerful. By that time Mama had practically convinced Rosie that she'd been wrong about hearing someone leave the house. Maybe it had been the Larsens' door that had slammed. Maybe the wind had flapped a shutter (even if there was no wind). No one was hiding in the house. Nothing was missing.

Her mother had had a harder time convincing her

father when he called the second time. Finally, after Mama had promised to have extra keys made and keep the doors locked, Rosie and her father talked again.

"I've been thinking about your problem," he said. "The piano problem. Have you thought up a story to go with the music?"

"Not yet." For the last hour Rosie hadn't even thought about "The Dance of the Dinosaurs." She'd been too busy searching for a burglar.

"Well, try it," he insisted, "first thing tomorrow. And I'm going to send you something else that might help. I can order it—them—from a store near my office."

He wouldn't tell her what the something else was, even though she begged and teased. When they said good-bye, they were both laughing.

Lightning leaped across the piece of sky framed by the bedroom window. Again and again it flared, brighter each time. The wardrobe loomed in the corner, looking even bigger than it did during the day. The flashes of light made it seem as if the doors might be opening, ever so slowly.

Rosie switched on the bedside lamp. The wardrobe doors were tightly closed, the bedroom cozy and snug.

"Rosie, why is your light on?" Her mother was calling from her room down the hall. "Is anything wrong?"

Rosie glanced at the little ivory alarm clock. Nine-thirty. "I wanted to see what time it is, that's all."

"Well, now you know. Go to sleep, hon."

As she switched off the light and settled back on her pillow, the wind set the curtains dancing. All at once, the thunder was directly overhead. Rain rattled across the roof.

"Close your window," Mama called again. "The floor will get soaked."

Rosie slipped out of bed and hurried across the room. The curtains flew straight out to meet her, and a cool spray touched her cheeks. She looked down into the thrashing, noisy darkness of the backyard. As she stared, an especially bright spear of lightning lit up the night. The blue light picked out the garage, the lilac bushes, the maple tree, and then a dark figure moving out from under the swaying branches.

Rosie closed the window with a crash and scampered back to bed. Had she really seen someone? She dived under the sheet where Bert Bear was waiting and hugged him close.

"There's someone in the backyard," she whispered. "I think. What'll we do?"

"Stay where we are," Bert whispered at once. "The house is locked up tight. We're safe. . . . Besides, I bet you imagined it."

"I didn't," Rosie argued. But she was glad to take the old bear's advice. After a long, heart-thumping time, she fell asleep.

By morning, the storm was over. The backyard looked fresh and inviting in the bright sunlight. Rosie stared down at the spot where she thought she'd seen the figure last night. It seemed silly now—a scary dream, that was all. Why would someone stand around in the backyard during a thunderstorm? She opened the window wide, smoothed the covers on her bed, and hurried downstairs for breakfast. She had work to do.

Making up a story to fit "The Dance of the Dinosaurs" was easy. First she played it through from beginning to end, listening intently to the loud, thumping chords and the lighter ripples of melody. There had to be an enormous dinosaur here in the first part, thumping his way around the beautiful valley where he lived. What was he doing? He was searching for food for himself and his wife dinosaur and his little daughter. She pictured him stamping boulders to bits as he walked and stretching to reach the leaves at the tops of the trees. But most of the food in the valley had been used up, and—*thump, thump*—the father dinosaur was unhappy. Here, in the slow, heavy part at the bottom of page two, he was telling his family he'd have to go somewhere else to look for food.

On the next two pages, the mother dinosaur and her little daughter searched for food themselves. They missed the father very much, but they were having fun while they searched. Rosie imagined them splashing through a river and playing hide-and-seek in a meadow full of flowers. The little dinosaur ducked her head in the tall grass so her mother couldn't find her.

The fifth page began with crashes and growls. That could be a thunderstorm, like the one last night. The dinosaurs were frightened, poor things. They hid in a cave, while the lightning flashed and the thunder rolled across the valley. There was a gentle melody at the bottom of the page; maybe that was the lullaby the mother sang to help her daughter go to sleep.

Rosie turned to the last page. *Thump, thump, thump*. Those loud chords must be the father dinosaur returning home with food for his family. Then came the long hard run that Rosie dreaded. How did it fit into the story? Well, the mother and daughter would surely hear the father's footsteps. What would they do? She smiled just thinking about it. They would *burst* out of the cave, so happy to see the father again that they would dance all the way up the mountain to the very top. She knew dinosaurs didn't dance or climb mountains, but *her* dinosaurs could do it. Down they'd come, full of joy. And all the time, the father dinosaur would be thumping around the valley, very pleased with himself and glad to be home.

Rosie turned back to page one and started telling herself the story again. She closed her eyes, and to her amazement she could see the notes behind her eyelids. Line by line they appeared, as she pictured what was happening to the dinosaur family. She played through the first three pages without looking at the music once.

"Rosie, that was wonderful!" her mother exclaimed from the doorway. "Simply great."

And it *was* great, right up to the last page. Then the nine fingers stumbled over each other, and the dance up and down the mountain ended with a crash.

Rosie bit her lip. Her father had helped her solve one problem, but the other one was still there. She played the run again and again, as slow as syrup dripping from a pitcher. The dinosaurs didn't sound happy, but at least she hit all the notes.

# CHAPTER 7

"What're you doing?"

Rosie peered over her mother's shoulder at the clutter on the kitchen table. There were photo albums, empty frames, portraits in their cardboard folders, and stacks of the envelopes the drugstore used to hold finished prints.

"Look at this." Mama held up a picture of Rosie and her father—an old picture, taken when Rosie was a fat baby and Papa had a mustache. "I'm matching up all my favorite photos with some of the old frames that were lying around in the attic. We're going to have a picture gallery in the upstairs hall. What do you think of that?"

"Okay, I guess."

Her mother turned and looked at her. "Can't you

sound a little more enthusiastic? It'll be a kind of picture history of this family." Rosie frowned, not sure why she didn't much like the idea.

"Does Papa know you're doing it?"

Her mother put down the scissors. "What an odd question, Rosie! I don't have to ask your father's permission to hang pictures. I enjoy fixing up this house. And when your father comes home, he'll be pleased."

That was it, Rosie thought. The family gallery would be another reason for staying in Dexter. Like the wardrobe. Her mother was piling up reasons why this house was perfect for them—little reasons that would add up to a big one.

*This is home.*

Rosie suddenly understood one of the reasons she hated the wardrobe. Besides the fact that it looked like a coffin, it had been brought in while her father was away. It was part of an argument, and he wasn't here to take the other side.

*Well,* she thought, *I don't want to move to Milwaukee any more than Mama does.* But what if moving was the only way her family would ever be together again? What then?

The telephone rang, and Rosie hurried to answer it. Maybe Angela wanted to go for a bike ride or to the library. Maybe she had another invitation for both of them to visit Mary Jean. Rosie snatched up the phone.

To her amazement, the caller was Mary Jean herself.

"It's my birthday on Saturday," she explained in her

small, cool voice. "I'm having a party and you're invited."

She paused, but Rosie was too excited to say a word.

"It's not a *real* party," Mary Jean went on. "I don't know many kids in Dexter so far. Just you and Angela and me." Another pause. "Okay?"

Rosie managed a choky "Fine."

"Come at noon," Mary Jean said, "so that we can have lunch. And bring your bathing suit. My father says the pool will be ready by then."

A birthday party. A swim in the new pool. Another chance to look at the dollhouse. The invitation sounded too good—too perfect—to be true.

Rosie's delight lasted through forty-five minutes of piano practice. It lasted through Angela's phone call and her offhand comment that Mary Jean had probably invited them because she didn't know anyone else. It even lasted through a boring drive to the mall to buy more frames for the picture gallery. Mama hardly spoke all the time they were in the car.

It wasn't till they were home again, and her mother had gone upstairs to start hanging pictures, that something happened to send the good feeling out the door.

"Rosie, for heaven's sake!" Mama sounded furious. "You come up here this minute."

Rosie climbed the stairs, trying to remember whether she'd made her bed or not. When her mother was cross or sad, it didn't take much to cause a real explosion.

Mama stood in the doorway of the bedroom, her hands on her hips. "What's the meaning of this?" she demanded.

The bedroom—at least one corner of it—was a mess. The wardrobe doors were wide open, and skirts and blouses were tumbled out on the floor. The big drawer at the bottom was open, too, and most of the shoes and board games Rosie had stored there were scattered across the floor.

"I'm surprised at you," Mama said. "You're not usually so careless. What's the use of having a beautiful piece for holding your things if you don't keep it neat?"

Rosie stared. "I didn't do that," she said. "I didn't even open the drawer today."

"Of course you did. You changed your shoes before we went shopping," Mama said sharply. "And you changed your T-shirt, too, because your yellow one had a hole under the arm."

"But I didn't leave stuff—"

"Now, what's the use of arguing? Who else could have done it? Just go ahead and straighten this up. And next time be more careful."

Rosie was frightened. She'd forgotten about changing before the trip to the mall, but she knew she hadn't left the wardrobe looking like this. Someone else had done it, a mysterious someone who must have sneaked in when they weren't at home. She started to ask whether the doors had been locked while they were gone, and then she stopped. She knew the answer. She and Mama had both forgotten about it. After all, nobody locked their doors in Dexter.

"I'll put the stuff away."

"Good." As suddenly as it had begun, the explosion was over. Mama put her hand on Rosie's head for just a second, and Rosie guessed that her mother was remembering the unlocked doors, too. "I'm sorry I yelled," she said. "Just a few clothes scattered around —there's nothing to be so upset about, I guess."

Rosie nodded.

"How about strawberry shortcake for supper?" Mama suggested. Next to chocolate cream pie, strawberry shortcake was Rosie's favorite dessert.

Rosie rolled her eyes and rubbed her tummy, even though she wasn't one bit hungry. She started picking up the shoes and games scattered across the bedroom floor. Mama watched for a moment and then went downstairs.

For the next half hour, Rosie could hear her mother walking through the house, opening and closing doors, and singing "The Battle Hymn of the Republic" to show she wasn't afraid of what she might find.

# CHAPTER 8

"I have a new bathing suit for the party," Angela bragged. "Wait'll you see it!" She patted the red tote bag between them.

Mrs. Carillo winked at Rosie in the rearview mirror. "You have a new bathing suit because the old one was too tight, young lady," she said. "We're going to have to put you on a diet before this summer is over."

"It's gorgeous." Angela grinned. "And I'm gorgeous in it."

Mrs. Carillo shook her head. "Such a modest child," she said. "My, my."

Rosie smiled contentedly. It had seemed as if Saturday would never come, but at last she was on her way to Mary Jean's birthday party. For a whole afternoon she could forget about burglars and "The Dance of the Dinosaurs." This afternoon she could be just like Mary Jean, with no problems at all.

Mary Jean opened the front door before they knocked. She led them through the house to the patio. Mr. Weiss was there, wearing khaki shorts and a T-shirt that said I AM THE COOK. He was tall and skinny, not a bit like Rosie's father, but seeing him cook hamburgers made her feel like crying. On Saturday, fathers were home from work and grilled hamburgers for their families. *Some* fathers. She managed a hello in answer to Mrs. Weiss's cheerful greeting and then hurried over to the edge of the pool. "We're going to have lunch before we swim," Mary Jean said, as if she thought Rosie might jump in with her clothes on. "Did you bring your bathing suit?"

"Of course she did," Angela shouted. She was up on the diving board, bouncing noisily. "Why don't we change right now? Then we'll be ready to swim after lunch."

"I've got my suit on under my shorts," Rosie said.

"You can't swim *right* after lunch," Mrs. Weiss told them as she came out of the house with a big platter of fruit. "You must give yourself time to digest your food." She set the platter on the glass-topped table and went to inspect the hamburgers. "What do you girls want to do until we're ready to eat? It'll be ten minutes or so."

Rosie knew what she'd like to do. She'd like to go

upstairs and look at the dollhouse. But before she could suggest it, Mrs. Weiss had a suggestion of her own. "I have an idea!" she exclaimed. "Why don't you play your recital pieces for each other? It will be good practice."

"Mo-ther," Mary Jean moaned, "nobody wants to do that. This is a party."

"I know, dear," Mrs. Weiss said apologetically. "I just thought it would be fun. . . ."

"Well, it wouldn't be," Mary Jean said.

"I can't play mine, anyway, Aunt Marcia," Angela said. "I haven't finished memorizing it. I don't know if I'm even going to be in the recital. Mrs. Kramer told Mom she might take me out if I didn't practice more."

"Oh, Angela!" Mrs. Weiss was shocked.

"I don't care," Angela said. "I'm sick of piano lessons. You know what I'd really like to play? Bagpipes!"

Mr. Weiss chuckled, and Mrs. Weiss shook her head. "How about you, Rosie?" she asked. "Will you play for us?"

Rosie put her hands behind her. What was happening to her perfectly perfect afternoon?

"I can't," she said softly. "I mean—I still have to practice some more."

"Well, I'm not going to play either," Mary Jean said crossly. "Not on my birthday. Besides, I don't need to practice any more. I know the whole thing. Let's go upstairs—"

A car door slammed, and footsteps pounded along the driveway at the side of the house.

"He was supposed to be gone till after lunch," Mary Jean said. "You promised!"

Her mother sighed. "Mrs. Driscoll said she'd take Eldon and her David for lunch at a hamburger place," she said. "I don't know—maybe they ate early. Don't worry, it'll be all right. . . ." She broke off as Eldon galloped into view. His hands and arms were gray with dirt, and he carried a small carton in one hand.

"Hello, dear, did you and David have a good time?" Mrs. Weiss tried to stop him as he passed her, but he ducked out of reach.

"Great!" he shouted. He raced across the patio, snatched a slice of watermelon from the center of the fruit platter, gave his sister a push, and kicked a beach ball into the middle of the pool. Mr. and Mrs. Weiss watched helplessly, and Mary Jean shrieked when he came near her again.

"Darling." Mrs. Weiss tried again to grab him. "Did Mrs. Driscoll take you and David out for lunch?"

"Yup." Eldon was gleeful. "Hamburgers and french fries and ice cream. We ate in the car, and David spilled but I didn't. Much. And then we went back to David's house and dug in the dirt."

"No kidding," Mary Jean muttered. "I never would have guessed *that*."

"I want to go swimming," Eldon said, whirling around. "I'm the best swimmer there is."

"Well, you can't go in now," Mary Jean shouted. "Not till we've had our lunch. You'd splash all over us. And you can't eat with us either—you've had enough."

Eldon glared at her. "I don't want to eat with you," he said. "I've got important work to do." He dashed into the house.

"What do you suppose—" Mrs. Weiss murmured.

"He's a great kid," Mr. Weiss said heartily. "Always busy. Always has some little project."

"He's disgusting," Mary Jean said. "When are we going to eat?"

Five minutes later they were seated around the glass table enjoying hamburgers, potato chips, and fruit. At first Rosie kept watching for Eldon to reappear, but then she settled down to enjoy the party. Finally, the afternoon was the way she'd imagined it would be. *We're like movie stars,* she thought, *sitting by our pool.*

"We'll have the birthday cake and ice cream later," Mrs. Weiss said, "after you've had your swim. Eldon will want some, too."

"Anybody ready for another hamburger?" Mr. Weiss asked. Rosie noticed that he and Mrs. Weiss kept glancing at Mary Jean, who continued to scowl.

"I'll have one," Angela said. "I could eat hamburgers forever."

"Me, too," Rosie agreed.

Mary Jean stared over their heads. "I like pizza

better," she said. "You promised Eldon wouldn't be here."

Rosie thought Mr. Weiss looked sad. He was a nice father, and he wanted Mary Jean to be happy on her birthday. She could imagine him at the piano recital clapping extra-hard for his daughter. Like her own father would, if he were there. The thought startled her. What if her father didn't come home for the recital? He wanted to, she knew, but what if he just couldn't because of his job? She hadn't let herself think about that before.

The thought stayed with her, like a toothache, till lunch was over. Then the girls went up to Mary Jean's bedroom. Rosie hurried straight to the dollhouse and stared into the beautiful little rooms.

"I like the cradle best," Angela said over her shoulder. "Look at the teeny-tiny blanket with a bunny stitched on it."

"My mother sewed the blanket," Mary Jean said indifferently. "She made the pillow, too." The pillow was the size of a dime.

Rosie couldn't decide what she liked best today. The window seat in the attic, of course. And the grand piano in the living room. Perhaps the glass-bead chandelier in the dining room. Or the little bathtub. . . . She screamed and jumped backward, almost knocking Angela down.

"There's something in the bathtub!" she squealed. "Something squirmy!"

Angela and Mary Jean crowded closer. "It's—it's a worm!" Mary Jean shrieked. "There's a worm in the bathtub!"

"Ugh, look!" Angela pointed at the largest of the dollhouse bedrooms. A long gray worm lay on the bed beneath the lacy canopy.

After that, they saw worms everywhere they looked. In the kitchen sink. On the velvet couch. In a tiny wastebasket. As Rosie stared in horror, the bunny blanket in the baby's cradle moved ever so slightly, and a worm poked its head—or maybe its tail—from under the ruffled edge.

*"Mother,"* Mary Jean howled. *"Daddy!* Look what he's done now."

By the time her parents arrived, Mary Jean was on her bed, roaring into her pillow.

"What's happened?" Mr. Weiss puffed. "Good grief, I thought someone was dead."

"Tell us, darling—" Mrs. Weiss turned from Mary Jean, who had begun kicking the blue ruffled bedspread and beating the pillow with her fists. "Girls, what *is* it?"

Wide-eyed, Rosie and Angela looked from Mary Jean to her parents. "In there." Rosie pointed into the dollhouse living room. "See?" An especially big worm was wiggling out from under the raised lid of the grand piano.

"Oh, no." Mrs. Weiss pressed her fingers to her forehead. "That boy! No, no, no."

Mr. Weiss stared as the worm crossed the living

room carpet, heading for the stairs. "We should have asked *why* he was digging in the dirt at David's house," he said after a moment. "We should re-member always to ask him *why.*"

# CHAPTER 9

They found ten more worms in the dollhouse.

"Here's one." Angela drew back quickly as a worm slithered out of the refrigerator.

Mr. Weiss opened the oven. "And one in here," he said. "Well, I think that does it. I'll just take all these fellows outside where they belong. They're perfectly harmless, you know," he added, looking at Mary Jean. "No need to cry, honey. It was just Eldon's little joke."

"I feel like crying," Mary Jean sobbed from her bed. "He's spoiled my dollhouse forever. I won't even be able to sleep in this room, thinking of all those awful worms crawling out of the house and coming over here to *get* me."

Rosie shuddered.

"Let's swim," Angela suggested. She was bored now that the worm hunt was over. "I want to try out my new suit."

"I don't want to swim," Mary Jean pouted. "Eldon probably put worms in the pool, too."

"Darling, of course he didn't," Mrs. Weiss protested. She'd been hovering at the foot of the bed, looking as if she'd like to give Mary Jean a hug but didn't dare. "Would you like me to search the dollhouse one more time—just so you'll be absolutely sure? Then you can all change into your swimming suits and have a wonderful time in the pool."

"I don't care," Mary Jean muttered. But she sat up in bed and watched while her mother examined each room of the dollhouse, opening drawers, picking up furniture. "You see? Everything's fine, dear. Not a sign...." Mrs. Weiss flicked open the tiny breadbox on the kitchen counter. She shut it swiftly, but not before Rosie saw an eye peering out.

Angela snatched up her red tote bag and ran into the bathroom. "Come on, Rosie," she shouted, "let's get ready."

When the door closed behind them they collapsed in a giggling heap.

"What was that thing in the breadbox?" Rosie whispered. "Not a worm."

"A teeny-tiny frog!" Angela clutched her stomach, trying to hold in the laughter. "He's something, isn't he?"

"The frog?"

"No, silly. Eldon."

There was a sharp rap on the door. "Are you changed?" Mary Jean demanded. "Hurry up."

Angela rolled her eyes.

"She sounds crabby," Rosie said. "What's the matter with her, anyway? *We* didn't put the worms in the dollhouse."

Angela pulled her new swimsuit from the bag. It was bright yellow. "She'll be all right," she whispered. "Just pretend not to notice. That's what everyone does around here."

When the girls returned to the bedroom, Mrs. Weiss was gone, and Mary Jean was sitting on the edge of the bed. She was wearing a blue swimsuit and making toe marks in the thick carpeting.

"Okay, let's go," she ordered, as if nothing unusual had happened.

Rosie and Angela followed her out to the stairs, both sneaking quick looks into the dollhouse kitchen as they passed. The breadbox was gone. Mrs. Weiss must have smuggled it out with her when she left, so Mary Jean wouldn't find out there had been still another uninvited guest at her party.

When they reached the backyard they saw that Eldon was already in the pool, splashing noisily at the shallow end. Mr. Weiss sat in a shady corner of the patio reading a magazine, and Mrs. Weiss was nowhere in sight.

"Cleaning the breadbox, I bet." Angela snickered under her breath.

Mary Jean went to the corner steps leading down into the water. She scowled at her brother, and Rosie wondered if the screaming and crying were going to start all over again. Mary Jean waded into the water, staying as far away from Eldon as she could. Rosie and Angela were right behind her.

Rosie ducked, and the blue water danced below her chin. The trouble with a swimsuit was that it had no pockets—no place to hide her hand. So far, the Weisses hadn't seemed to notice her missing finger, but maybe they were just being polite. She particularly didn't want Eldon to notice. Who could guess what mean thing he might do or say!

It was Rosie's first swim of the summer. Last year she and her mother and father had gone out to Eagle Lake several times. Mama, who was an expert swimmer, had taught Rosie to float and do a simple crawl. She wondered if she could still do them.

She flipped over on her back, and water filled her nose and eyes. It had been easier when she knew her mother's hand was beneath her, ready to hold her up. Having her father nearby, cheering, had helped, too. She tried it again, lying back more slowly this time, bringing up her legs, letting her head slip into the water as if she were resting on a pillow.

Good!

The water lapped over her ears, cutting off the other swimmers' squeals as they waded deeper into the pool. She closed her eyes. For a moment she could believe it really was last summer, and she and

Mama and Papa were in the water together, with Bert Bear waiting and watching next to the picnic basket on the beach.

"Rosie!" Water splashed her face, and the daydream vanished. Mary Jean was beside her, bobbing up and down with impatience. "Show me how to float," she demanded. "I want to do it, too."

"Me, too," Angela shouted. She pretended to swim toward them, making wild splashing motions with her arms as she waded. Beyond her Eldon circled closer. *Like a little shark,* Rosie thought nervously. He hadn't even looked at them at first, but now he seemed ready to join the party.

"Don't let me go," Mary Jean ordered, as ripples broke across her face. "Keep your hand under my back, Rosie."

The little shark was very close now. Rosie wished Mr. Weiss would look up from his magazine. Suddenly Eldon ducked underwater and came up next to Mary Jean's feet. He grabbed one of his sister's ankles and pulled.

"Don't!" Rosie shrieked. Angela tried to grab Eldon's arm and missed. Before he let go, Mary Jean's head was underwater, and her feet were pounding the air. Rosie tried to help and was pulled underwater for a second, herself. Angela screamed.

"What's going on over there?" Mr. Weiss called. "Don't play rough, kids."

Mary Jean bobbed to the surface. She was crying again.

"Make him stop!" she wailed. "Make him get out of the pool, Daddy!"

*I wouldn't cry if Eldon were my brother,* Rosie thought fiercely. *I'd push him underwater and see how he liked it.* She waited to see what Mr. Weiss would do.

"Mustn't tease the girls, son," he said. "That's a good fella."

Mrs. Weiss came out on the patio. Maybe *she* would make Eldon behave—but Rosie doubted it. "Remember he's just a little boy," she said sweetly. "We have to have patience, don't we?" She smiled at them all and went back inside.

Mary Jean took a blubbery breath. "He never gets blamed for anything," she sobbed. "Never! He tried to drown me and he put worms in my dollhouse and—" She swept an enormous wave in the direction of her grinning little brother. "If you get near me again, you'll be sorry," she threatened. "I mean it."

Eldon's smile faded. "I didn't do anything," he whined. "You're supposed to play with me."

"I'd rather play with—with a hornet!" Mary Jean turned to Rosie. "I want to try to float again. I almost had it." She shot her brother a furious look. "Angie, you watch *him* and tell me if he comes close."

Angela reached for the beach ball floating near the edge of the pool. "Come on, Eldon," she shouted, "let's play ball."

"No!" Mary Jean shrieked. "Don't play with him. He's too awful." She snatched the ball out of Angela's hands and tossed it aside. "Just watch him," she said. "Come on, Rosie, put your hand under my back."

"Okay," Rosie said. She looked at Angela.

"Okay." Angela shrugged. "But watching's no fun."

On her next try, Mary Jean floated easily. "I'm doing it!" she exclaimed. "I can float. Look at me."

"Looks dumb," Eldon sneered.

Rosie took her hand away and stepped back. She leaned forward into the glittering water. Her feet drifted upward until she lay facedown on the surface. Below her the white tiles rippled like squares of silk. It was nice, she thought—this bright, silent world. Eldon's tricks and Mary Jean's tears seemed far away.

The peaceful view vanished in a storm of bubbles. Something smacked Rosie's side and then fastened on her leg, pushing her upward and tipping her till her hands touched the tiles. Startled, she kicked as hard as she could and broke away from whatever it was that had pushed her to the bottom. When she came up, gasping for air, Eldon was a couple of feet away. Blood streamed from his nose.

"You kicked me!" he roared. "Daddy, I'm all bloody!"

"I couldn't stop him," Angela said, splashing toward Rosie. "He's so darned fast."

Mr. Weiss hurried to the side of the pool. "Come out of the water, son," he urged. Rosie tried to help, but the little boy jerked away. Angela took his hand

and drew him to the edge of the pool so his father could lift him out.

"Rosie didn't kick him on purpose, Uncle Jack," she said earnestly. "Eldon pushed her underwater. She was just trying to get away."

"I didn't do anything," Eldon wailed. "That girl is bad!"

"Serves him right," Mary Jean shrieked. "Now maybe he'll leave us alone."

Mr. Weiss sat down with Eldon on his lap, not seeming to notice the wetness. He tilted the little boy's head back to stop the bleeding and wiped his face with a handkerchief.

"I'm sorry," Rosie said softly. "I didn't mean to kick him. I just got scared."

"Things happen," Mr. Weiss said. But he held Eldon closer, as if he'd do anything in the world to keep things from happening to *him*. "Poor little guy."

"He's not a poor little guy," Mary Jean said. "He's the worst pest who ever lived."

Rosie stood very still, wanting Mr. Weiss to say he knew the kick was just an accident, wanting him to say Rosie wasn't a bad person. Instead, he stood up after a moment and carried Eldon into the house.

"Good," Mary Jean shouted after them, "now we can have some fun!" She grabbed Rosie's hand—the right one—then dropped it. "Oh, yuk!" she exclaimed. "Your fingers—" She stared, her face suddenly closed up and strange. "What's wrong with your hand?"

Rosie thrust the hand behind her and stared back. She couldn't speak. The last person to notice had been the man who delivered the wardrobe, and she'd been able to answer *his* questions with no trouble at all. This was different. How could she tell Mary Jean that a missing finger didn't matter, when, obviously, Mary Jean thought it was *disgusting?*

"So she's got nine fingers," Angela said, "so what?" She was looking anxiously from Rosie to Mary Jean, all three of them standing like statues in the dancing blue water.

Mary Jean shrugged. "Sure," she said uncertainly, "so what?"

"Let's play pickle-in-the-middle," Angela shouted. She tossed the beach ball to Rosie, but Rosie didn't catch it. She still had her hand behind her back. "I'm tired of swimming," she said, backing away from the big, bobbing ball. "I'm going to dry off."

She backed all the way to the pool steps and climbed out onto the cream-colored tiles.

"Come on," Angela begged, "we can have fun."

Rosie shook her head and stretched out in the sun. She *was* tired of swimming, but that wasn't all. She was tired of this whole, long, not-so-perfect party.

# CHAPTER 10

"Anyway, the birthday cake was yummy," Angela said. "You liked the cake, didn't you, Rosie?"

Rosie nodded.

"And the ice cream shaped like musical notes. That was neat."

Rosie nodded again. Now that she was almost home, she could begin to think about the good parts of the afternoon.

"Mary Jean loved the bracelet you gave her," Angela went on. "She said she's going to wear it to the recital next week. It was a whole string of little silver elephants," she told her mother. "Mary Jean put it on right away. She didn't like my present at all."

"Well, nobody gets very excited about a petticoat," Mrs. Carillo said calmly. "But Mary Jean needed a new one—Aunt Marcia told me. And she can wear that to the recital, too." She cocked an eyebrow at Angela. "What's the matter? Rosie's quiet as a mouse, and you sound as if you're trying to convince her that she had a good time. What happened?"

Neither girl answered. After a moment, Mrs. Carillo gave a little shrug and turned on the car radio.

"Call you tomorrow," Rosie said, when they pulled up in front of her house. "Thanks for the ride, Mrs. Carillo."

"Let's have a picnic Monday," Angela shouted after her. Rosie turned and waved to show she'd heard.

A fresh, sharp smell met her at the front door. She followed it through the house and found Mama in the kitchen painting cupboards. Half of the old gray cupboards were now a beautiful sunny yellow. There was a matching yellow streak across her mother's forehead.

"I didn't know you were going to paint," Rosie said. "It's pretty."

Mama looked hot and tired. "I just decided to do it this afternoon," she said. "Did you have a good time at the party?"

"It was okay." Rosie watched the paintbrush sweep along the edge of another cupboard door. She waited for the million questions that were sure to follow, but her mother didn't seem to be thinking about anything but the paint. "I hope this dries," she said. "It's so awfully hot out."

The daisy-and-butterfly cookie jar had been moved to the kitchen table so paint wouldn't drip on it. Rosie took out two gingersnaps and nibbled them while she watched her mother work. *Everything's changing,* she thought. *The kitchen cupboards are yellow and the upstairs hall is full of pictures and there's the wardrobe in my bedroom.* She wished the cupboards were still gray, even though the yellow was much prettier.

"Your father called just after you left for the party. He was sorry he missed you."

Rosie felt a sharp stab of disappointment. She hated to miss a chance to talk to him. "Did he say anything special?"

"He said he's sent you a present to help with your recital piece. I can't imagine what it is. He mailed it a couple of days ago, so it might get here today."

Rosie couldn't guess either. "I meant, did he say anything about—you know—coming home. For the recital."

Her mother tilted back on her bare heels and narrowed her eyes at the gleaming cupboard door. "That wasn't what he called about," she said slowly. "He called to say he's found a house he likes in Milwaukee. He wants us to come and look at it. He wants to buy it."

Rosie's stomach did a wild flip-flop. Buying a house in Milwaukee meant staying there. It meant her father didn't intend to move back to Dexter—ever.

And she was sure her mother wouldn't move to

Milwaukee. That was why she'd decided to paint the kitchen this afternoon. It was another way of saying NO!

"When are we going to see the house?" Rosie asked. "Maybe it's real nice. Maybe—"

The paintbrush began another sweep. "I told him we wouldn't be coming," Mama said in a shaky voice. "I'm sure it's a nice house—your father has good taste. But this is home." She dropped the brush in the paint can and twisted around to give Rosie a hug. "Don't look so worried, sweetie," she said. "It'll work out. He'll come to his senses, and then we'll be together again."

The front doorbell rang. "I'll go," Rosie offered. She didn't want to talk about what was going to happen, and she didn't want to watch that paintbrush moving back and forth. With every stroke, her father seemed farther away.

When she reached the front door, a delivery truck was just pulling away from the curb. A big box stood on the porch next to the pot of geraniums. It was addressed to Miss Rosie Carpenter, Pianist, First Class.

She carried the box to the kitchen. Mama stopped painting to help her cut the tape that sealed the cover.

"It's so light," Rosie said. "Maybe he forgot to put the present inside."

Her mother shook her head. "Not your father." She folded back the flaps, uncovering lots of crumpled green tissue paper. "Reach in and see if you can guess what it is without looking."

Rosie plunged her arm into the box. Her hand closed on something soft and smooth. She pulled the object out of the box, scattering tissue paper balls over the table.

"It's—it's a dinosaur!" Rosie said. "A stuffed dinosaur in a green straw hat!"

Mama giggled. "In *my* green straw hat," she said. "Don't you recognize it? That's just like the big floppy hat I wear to work in the garden. Your father must have made it. Why in the world would he do that?"

Rosie reached into the tissue paper again and pulled out another dinosaur. This one was bigger. Eyeglasses of twisted wire were taped to his head, and a little wooden pipe stuck out of his mouth.

"That's Papa!" Rosie shouted. "He made a mother and father dinosaur." She dived into the box with both hands, and the rest of the tissue paper went flying.

"There can't be *another* one," her mother said. But there was.

Rosie set the smallest dinosaur between the other two. The littlest dinosaur had a bright red bow taped between its ears.

"That man!" Mama exclaimed. "That's what I loved about him first—his sense of humor." She didn't look nearly as tired and unhappy as she had a few minutes ago.

Rosie gathered up the three dinosaurs and carried them into the living room. They belonged on the piano where she could see them every time she played "The Dance of the Dinosaurs." She wondered how Papa had guessed that she would make up a story about a mother and father dinosaur and their daughter.

"That man!" Mama said again. "What a funny idea!" She and Rosie looked at the dinosaurs for a minute, and then she turned back to the kitchen. "Come on, let's make supper," she said. "You can tell me about the birthday party. Did Mary Jean like your present?"

"She liked it a lot," Rosie said. "She's going to wear it to the recital."

"That's nice." Mama looked around the half-painted kitchen. "We'll have to eat out on the porch, I suppose," she said. "The paint smell is too strong in here."

Rosie didn't care where they ate. She wasn't very hungry. Maybe it was the birthday cake and ice cream, or maybe it was the scary thought that had come with the dinosaurs. What if Papa had sent them for a special reason? What if he wanted Rosie to know that he would like to come to the recital himself, but couldn't? Maybe the dinosaur family was supposed to take his place.

# CHAPTER 11

When Rosie and Angela had a picnic, they almost always went to the same place. Today they walked up to the corner nearest Rosie's house and turned left without hesitating. The county highway and the Gabels' farm were only ten minutes away.

"I'm not going to be in the recital," Angela announced, after they'd walked for a while. She held out her bag of popcorn.

Rosie helped herself. "You have to be in it," she protested. "Everybody has to be in it who takes lessons."

"Wrong! Mrs. Kramer told me I was out this morning. If you don't learn your recital piece by heart, you can't be on the program. I only know the first page." Angela stuffed another handful of popcorn into her mouth and rolled her eyes at the memory.

"What did your mother and father say?"

"They said it was up to me. They said if I didn't work hard then I deserved to miss the Big Moment. That's what my mother calls the recital—the Big Moment. Ugh!"

Rosie wondered if the same thing was about to happen to her. She thought about this morning's practice session. With the help of the story she'd made up, and the dinosaur family ranged across the top of the piano, the memorizing had gone well. But that difficult run on the last page got worse instead of better. She couldn't play it smoothly, no matter how many times she tried. Each time she started the final section, a scolding voice—Mrs. Kramer's, perhaps—sounded in her ear.

*Silly girl! With only nine fingers, you know you can't play anything hard!*

And then came Mary Jean's shocked whisper—*Oh, yuk! Your fingers—*

"No!" The word slipped out before Rosie could stop it.

"No, what?" Angela asked.

"No, I don't want to drop out of the recital. I don't! I thought I might want to, but I don't."

Angela scooped out the last of the popcorn. "Nobody's asked *you* to drop out, have they? You like playing the piano. I hate it. That's a big difference."

They walked on. The houses became fewer, separated by fields of grass and wildflowers. A breeze lifted the grass in waves. Rosie forced herself to stop thinking about "The Dance of the Dinosaurs." The recital was six days away, and today was the picnic. *Enjoy the moment,* her father always said, when he lived at home.

"There she is," Angela said suddenly. "Did you bring her treat?"

Rosie reached into her lunch bag and brought out an apple. Angela had two carrots. Waiting for them, as if she'd known they were coming, was the silver-colored mare who had lived in Gabels' meadow as long as they could remember. The horse nosed the treats the girls held out and then lifted the apple from Rosie's hand.

"She must be the oldest horse in the world," Rosie said, petting the silvery neck. "And the nicest."

The horse bobbed her head as if she agreed. Then she took Angela's carrots and followed the girls as they waded through the grass to the huge oak tree in the center of the meadow.

"Maybe the raft is gone," Angela said. "Maybe Mr. Gabel hauled it away."

"It's there," Rosie said, before she could see it. The raft had to be there. It was where they always sat to have their picnics.

She was right. The raft—really an old barn door—was right where it belonged, in the shade of the oak. The girls called it their raft because when they sat there it was easy to pretend the grass around them was an ocean—an ocean full of sharks and octopuses and man-eating monsters. Angela jumped onto the boards and threw herself down on the sun-warmed wood. Rosie checked to make sure there weren't any spiders or other crawly creatures resting there, and then she lay down, too.

"I love it here," she said softly. "When I'm an old, old lady, I'm going to remember how nice this was."

"You're funny," Angela said, rolling over on her back. "We'll never be old, old ladies."

They ate lunch right away, because being on the raft made them hungry, even if they'd just finished a whole sack of popcorn. Rosie had her favorite cheese-and-pickle sandwiches, and Angela had peanut butter and jelly. They both had bottles of soda, and both had brought cookies—two apiece so they could trade. The silver-colored horse waited nearby, watching for the crusts the picnickers would throw into the "water."

When they had finished eating they stretched out on the raft again. The wood smelled like horses.

"Let's pretend we're sleeping and a shark is sneaking up on us," Angela murmured. "Or a person. Pretend there's a burglar swimming up to the raft to steal our jewels."

In spite of the warmth of the sun, Rosie shivered. She was thinking of the dark figure under the maple tree in her backyard. "I don't want to pretend there's a burglar," she said. "I *hate* burglars."

She hadn't intended to tell Angela about the strange things that had been happening at her house. Talking about them made them more real. But now she found herself telling the whole story in a small, sleepy voice —the back door that closed when no one should have been in the house, the figure in the backyard, the way her wardrobe had been opened and emptied. When she'd finished the story, she opened her eyes a crack and saw Angela sitting up straight, staring at her.

"Oh, wow, Rosie! You are so lucky! A mystery in your very own house!"

Rosie frowned. She didn't feel lucky.

"Listen," Angela said, "we've got to catch whoever it is. Let's make a plan." She leaned forward and hugged her knees with excitement.

Now Rosie was wide-awake. What had she started! Once Angela had a plan, she never gave it up.

"I know!" Angela exclaimed. "We'll hide in your house when your mother goes out and wait to see who comes in."

"Mama will never let us do that," Rosie said. "She'll say it's too dangerous."

"She won't even know," Angela said. "By the time she gets home, we'll know who the burglar is, and she'll thank us for being so smart."

"She locks the doors when she goes out," Rosie said. "No one can sneak in anymore."

"You can unlock them."

Rosie was shocked. "But that would be sort of like inviting the burglar to come in."

"Well, sure," Angela drawled, "we have to help him a little. How else are we going to find out who it is? Don't you want to stop your mom from worrying?" She jumped to her feet. "Let's go back to your house right now. Maybe she's gone someplace this afternoon. You have a key, don't you? We can sneak in and hide and—"

"She's home," Rosie said. "The plumber is coming to fix the leak in the bathtub."

"Well, then, we'll do it Wednesday." Angela hunkered down again, her eyes sparkling. "Wednesday's your piano lesson, right?"

Rosie sighed. "Right."

"Okay, here's what you do. You ask your mom to go with you. Mrs. Kramer will want to make sure you remember how to curtsy after you play and all that dumb stuff. Tell your mother you want her to watch. Leave your front door unlocked, and as soon as you're gone, I'll sneak in and hide. If the burglar comes, I'll get a good look at him. And then," she ended triumphantly, "we'll report him to the police. We'll probably get a medal."

"But what if he sees you?" Rosie protested. "He might—he might—" Her tongue refused to say what he might do, and at that moment the old horse whinnied impatiently. Both girls jumped, then giggled. Rosie gathered the remains of their lunch and tossed the scraps into the grass.

"The burglar won't see me," Angela said. "I'm a very good hider."

They argued about the plan all the way home, but when they turned the corner onto Rosie's street, the argument ended. A police car was parked in front of the old gray house.

"Something's wrong!" Rosie gasped. "Let's run!"

"I bet they've already caught him," Angela groaned.

They had nearly reached the house when a policeman came out on the porch. Rosie's mother followed him. She was very pale.

"Here come my daughter and her friend now," she said, "but I don't think Rosie can tell you anything more."

"What happened?" Rosie puffed. "Are you okay, Mama?"

Her mother smiled tiredly. "Of course I am. But I went to the grocery store while Mr. Bennett—the plumber—was working on the tub. While I was gone, he heard footsteps downstairs, and when he called, whoever it was ran out the back door. So we called the police."

The policeman sat in the porch swing and stretched out his long legs. "Your mother says you heard someone run out the back once before when you came in the front door," he said. "And you found your clothes tumbled around on the floor another time. Is there anything else that's happened?"

Rosie described the dark figure she'd seen under the tree in the backyard during the storm. "At least, I *think* someone was there," she said, not looking at Mama. "It was so dark. . . . "

"Anything else?"

Rosie shook her head.

"Well," the policeman said, standing up, "it does look as if somebody's interested in getting in here. Not a professional thief, I guess. He doesn't bother to check the front of the house before sneaking in the back—otherwise he'd have seen the plumber's truck today. And it doesn't seem as if whoever-it-is wants to come in if he thinks you're at home. I'd suggest that you lock up carefully every time you leave, and maybe that'll be the end of it. We'll drive by often and keep an eye on the place."

"Thank you," Mama said. "I wish you would."

"Anything else I can do for you?"

Angela spoke for the first time. "May I hold your gun?"

The policeman grinned at her. "No, you can't." He waved a good-bye and strolled down the walk to his car.

As soon as he was gone, Mama sank into the swing. "I really can't stand this," she said. "I can't handle some *creature* trying to get into our house every time our backs are turned. And why didn't you tell me you saw someone in the backyard, Rosie?" She gave the swing a hard push that sent it crashing into the house. "Somebody has to do something. I can't do it all myself."

Rosie knew what Mama meant. Her mother thought Papa should come home and catch the burglar.

She felt a sharp elbow dig into her ribs. "Somebody has to do something," Angela hissed. "And that somebody is us."

This time Rosie didn't argue.

# CHAPTER 12

Rosie couldn't remember a time when she'd purposely done something that would make her mother *furious* if she found out. She'd broken rules, of course. She usually threw away or traded the peaches in her school lunch because she hated the fuzzy skins. She let her homework go till the last minute, and she had once climbed nearly to the top of the maple tree in the backyard after being told never to go beyond the first big branch. But sneaking back to unlock the front door when Mama had locked it was different. It felt wicked.

"Come on, Rosie," Mama urged, leading the way across the backyard to the garage, "you act as if you're going to prison instead of to your piano lesson. Where's that smile?"

She was trying to sound cheerful, but Rosie had a

feeling her mother's mind was a long way from the music lesson—in Milwaukee, probably. It was just as well, because when they drove out into the street, there was Angela, barely hidden behind the elm tree. Rosie could see the tips of her red sandals and a big brown-paper bag next to her feet.

She wondered where her friend would hide after she'd unlocked the back door for the burglar. The hall closet next to the kitchen would be the best hiding place, because from there you could see anyone who came in.

"The thing is," Mama said after a few minutes, showing that she'd been thinking about the piano lesson after all, "you have the whole piece down very well, except for that last page. Except for that long run, actually. I can't quite see why that stops you. Is it because—" She stopped, not wanting to mention the Finger Problem. That was what she called it, if she had to mention it at all.

The Finger Problem showed how different her mother and her father were, Rosie thought. Papa said, *So you're short a finger. So what? There's nothing wrong with your head, kiddo, and that's what matters. Besides, nine fingers are enough.* Mama wanted to think Rosie was perfect, so she pretended the Finger Problem didn't exist.

"I don't know why I can't do it," Rosie said. "I just get scared every time I get to that part."

The car turned onto Main Street. "Maybe if you played it much slower. . . . "

"It's supposed to go fast," Rosie said stubbornly.

Mrs. Kramer's house looked different, now that the recital was just a few days off. It looked like a place where something scary might happen. The curving walk was very long, and the doorbell was terribly loud.

"Are you sure you want me to go in with you?" Mama asked. "I can wait at home and come back to pick you up in an hour."

"You have to come in," Rosie said. "Mrs. Kramer might want to tell you something important about the recital."

Mrs. Kramer did seem pleased that Rosie's mother had come. She showed them how the grand piano would be moved to the end of the long parlor, leaving room for rows of folding chairs. She reminded Rosie that she must curtsy at the end of her piece and made her practice doing it. Then she brought out the program, neatly typed on stationery with musical notes across the top. "The Dance of the Dinosaurs" was second to the last, just before Mary Jean's "Nocturne."

"My daughter will make copies of this later today," Mrs. Kramer said. She looked over the program proudly. "Of course, after that there can't be any changes. I've already had one student fail me. . . ."

"Well, you don't have to worry about Rosie," Mama said firmly. "You're going to do just fine, aren't you, hon?"

Rosie pretended to be studying the program. A few weeks ago she'd dreamed of seeing "The Dance of the Dinosaurs" at the very bottom. Rosie Carpenter, Star! Now she was relieved that Mary Jean had been given last place. This way, when Rosie Carpenter played badly, it wouldn't spoil the whole recital.

"Well, then," Mrs. Kramer exclaimed, too heartily, "let's hear those dinosaurs dance!" She took back the program and laid it on a coffee table.

Mama settled in a chair to listen. Mrs. Kramer sat on the piano bench next to Rosie.

The first thing to do was to imagine the dinosaur family lined up on top of the piano, the way they were at home. That helped. Rosie began to play, letting the story move through her mind. Line by line, page by page, the music flowed. She could feel Mrs. Kramer relax beside her.

She reached the last page, the end of the story. The mother and daughter dinosaurs were wildly happy because the father had come home at last. If only she could do it right this time!

"Slow down, Rose," Mrs. Kramer whispered, "not so fast."

But this part was supposed to be fast—loud and happy and fast. Rosie clenched her teeth and plunged ahead. Up the mountain, partway down—and she stopped.

"Begin the run again," Mrs. Kramer ordered. "You mustn't play it so fast."

Rosie began again, and this time she didn't even get to the top of the mountain. She looked at Mrs. Kramer with angry tears in her eyes.

"I have to work on it some more," she said. "At home. By myself."

She heard Mama sigh.

"I want you to play it now, Rose," Mrs. Kramer insisted. "And I want you to play it slowly—*very* slowly, if necessary."

"It's supposed to go fast," Rosie argued. "It says so on the music."

"I know that, dear," Mrs. Kramer said, "but you must play it the best way *you* can. You'll have to play it more slowly, or you're going to stumble. I think we've proved that."

Mary Jean Weiss would be able to play it fast, but Rosie Carpenter could not. That's what Mrs. Kramer was really saying. *The poor girl can't play a fast run with only nine fingers, and that's that!*

Rosie started the last page again. When she came to the run, she played it very, very slowly. The mother dinosaur and the little dinosaur dragged themselves up the mountain and down, up and down.

"Well, that's better," Mrs. Kramer said, but she didn't sound as if she meant it. "You play it that way, and we'll have nothing to worry about."

Rosie opened her mouth to say she would never play it that way. The run sounded terrible—like boring practice scales. But before she could say a word, Mama stood up.

"I think Rosie is tired," she said. "She needs to think about something else for a while. Like a new dress for the recital."

Mrs. Kramer stood up, too, even though barely half an hour of the lesson time had passed. "That's a fine idea," she said. "I'm sure you'll play all right on Saturday, Rose. Don't worry about it."

Rosie felt silent messages going back and forth between Mama to Mrs. Kramer. They felt sorry for her.

"Where shall we go to find the dress?" Mama asked, as soon as they were outside. "The Bandbox has pretty things. Or maybe that new store next to the bank?"

"I don't want a new dress," Rosie said. She took a deep breath. "I don't want to be in the recital. I can't play that last page."

There. The truth was out. Rosie had known it would be hard to admit there was something she couldn't do with nine fingers, but she wasn't ready for the wave of sadness that swept over her. How many other exciting things would she never be able to do?

"Of course you can play it," Mama said, giving her a hug. "You still have a couple more days to practice, hon. By Saturday it'll be fine. Now let's not talk about it anymore, okay? We have important shopping to do. Your father said he wants you to have a new dress—you've worn the pink-and-white stripe long enough."

Her father! "Do you think he's coming home for the recital?" It would be twice as hard to drop out—ten times as hard—if *he* tried to persuade her to play.

"I don't know," Mama said. "He'll come if he can, but Milwaukee's a long way off, and he wouldn't be able to leave until Saturday morning. You mustn't count on it."

They parked across the street from the Bandbox, and Mama led the way into the store, pretending not to notice Rosie's dragging feet.

"This'll be fun," she said. "You haven't had a new dress in a long time."

Rosie scowled. She kept on scowling when the clerk brought out a pale pink dress with rows of ruffles on the full skirt. The scowl deepened at the light blue taffeta with a wide lace collar.

"Maybe if you tried them on . . .?" the clerk urged.

Rosie shoved her fist deeper into the pocket of her jeans. "I don't like dresses like that," she said. "I don't like ruffles."

"Maybe that red one," Mama suggested. "You like red."

The clerk lifted a red corduroy dress from the rack and held it up. It was as bright as a Fourth of July balloon, with a dropped waist and a neat white collar. No ruffles. No lace.

In spite of herself, Rosie felt her frown slip away.

"Try it on," Mama coaxed. "This one looks right."

Staring at her bright-red self in the mirror, Rosie forgot for a moment that she didn't want to be in the recital.

"It's perfect," Mama said. "You like it, don't you?"

Rosie nodded. If she *were* going to play in the recital, this was the dress she would want to wear.

On the way to the car, Mama chattered in the phony-cheerful tone she'd been using ever since they left Mrs. Kramer's house. "As soon as we get home, you'd better call Angela," she said gaily. "She'll want to come over to see your new dress."

Rosie stopped in the middle of the sidewalk and stared at her mother. She'd forgotten all about Angela. Was she still hiding, waiting for the burglar to sneak back into Rosie's house? And what if he had come? What if—oh, what if he'd caught her spying on him?

Rosie grabbed her mother's hand. "Let's hurry," she begged. "I want to go home."

"Well, for heaven's sake," Mama laughed, but she let herself be hustled along.

All the way home, Rosie didn't say a word. When the car turned onto her street, she looked up the block fearfully. She half-expected to see a police car in front of the house again, or maybe Angela chasing a burglar across the neighbors' lawns. But the street was quiet.

Mama parked in front of the house instead of turning into the driveway. "You run ahead," she said. Rosie realized her mother thought she was in a hurry because she had to go to the bathroom. "Do you have your key?"

Rosie nodded and jumped out of the car. She

wouldn't need her key unless Angela had become tired of playing detective and had gone home. If she'd left, she would have remembered to turn the lock behind her.

But the door was unlocked. Rosie hurried inside and darted down the hall to the closet. "Angela, we're home! You'd better go before—" She flung open the door of the closet and peered inside. There was nothing there but brooms, a mop, and the vacuum cleaner. She raced back to the front hall and up the stairs. Behind her, Mama was opening the front door.

Rosie dived into the bathroom at the top of the stairs. She needed time to think. If Angela was still hiding in the house, she had to be smuggled out before Mama saw her.

"Honey, are you all right?" Her mother was just outside the bathroom door.

"I'm fine, Mama," Rosie bellowed. *Get out, Angela, get out!*

"I'll hang up the new dress," Mama said. Her footsteps tap-tapped down the hall to Rosie's room.

*Now, Angela!* Rosie tried again to send a message through the bathroom door. *Run!*

There was a thud, followed by a startled silence. Then, to Rosie's horror, her mother began to scream. Over and over, the shrill sounds echoed through the house.

Rosie opened the bathroom door. The burglar was in her bedroom—nothing else could make Mama scream like that. He'd murdered Angela, and now he was going to kill Mama! Rosie snatched up the toilet brush—the only weapon within reach—and ran down the hall.

The scene in her room was terrifying. Mama was crouched against the bed, sobbing, the new dress crushed beneath her. One of the wardrobe doors stood open, and Angela lay half inside, half out. Her eyes were wide and staring, and the front of her T-shirt was soaked with blood.

# CHAPTER 13

"Look, Mrs. Carpenter! Please! Look!" Angela jumped up and down. "I'm okay, see?" She made punching motions to show how healthy she was.

Rosie's mother lay facedown on the bed. Her face was buried in her arms, and she was still crying, but more quietly now. The deep, shuddery sobs were as frightening to Rosie as her mother's screams had been.

"Mama, *please,*" she begged, "look at Angela. She's not dead."

Actually, Angela didn't look well at all. The red stuff on her shirt front was enough like blood to be scary, even though Rosie knew now that it was only a strawberry Popsicle that had melted messily when Angela fell asleep in the wardrobe.

Mama refused to turn over, or pay any attention at all to their pleas. She had changed completely from the cheerful person who couldn't wait to buy Rosie a new dress.

"Why did you have to hide in the wardrobe, anyway?" Rosie demanded in a low voice. "How'd you expect to see the burglar with the doors closed?"

Angela gave her a dirty look. "The doors weren't closed at first, silly. I thought it was a good place to hide, because the burglar had already looked for your jewels and stuff in there, so he wouldn't look again. I was going to peek out when I heard him coming, and then I was going to get out and follow him. It wasn't my fault that the doors accidentally closed so I was trapped. What was I supposed to do except relax and eat my Popsicle and my popcorn—"

"You had popcorn, too?"

"And a chocolate bar, if you want to know. Being a detective is hard work. And boring. You were gone such a long time, and it got stuffy in the wardrobe, even though there's a crack under the door. You would have fallen asleep, too, if you'd been in there." She turned back to Rosie's mother. "Mrs. Carpenter, please don't cry anymore."

"Mama." Rosie was trying not to cry herself. "We wanted to help. Angela was going to find out who the burglar was and—"

"And get shot if he happened to be carrying a gun!" Her mother rolled over and sat up at last. Her face was red and her eyes puffy, the face of a stranger. "I am so angry with you two, I can't find words. I can't find words for *anything*. I'm fed up with burglars and plumbers and being in charge and—all of it." She threw herself back on the bed, facing the wall.

Rosie and Angela exchanged looks, their cross words forgotten. They hovered next to the bed, not knowing what to do, until the telephone rang downstairs. Rosie dashed out of the bedroom, grateful for a chance to escape.

The caller was Angela's mother. "Rosie, have you seen that girl of mine?" she asked. "She's been gone all afternoon. Just wandered off without a word. I'm sure she's all right but—"

"She's here," Rosie said quickly. It was comforting to hear Mrs. Carillo's kind, sensible voice. "We don't know what to do. My mother's crying because she thought Angela was dead—" There was a horrified gasp on the other end of the line. "Angela's okay," Rosie hurried on, "but Mama *thought* she was dead because of the Popsicle, and now she's all upset and she won't talk to us."

"I'll be right there," Mrs. Carillo said and hung up.

Rosie went out on the back porch and sat on the end of the couch. She could imagine Angela's mother dashing out of the house and cutting across backyards, following the same shortcuts Angela used.

When she forced herself to go back upstairs, Angela was coming down. "Your mom went into her bedroom and closed the door," Angela reported. "She says she wants to be alone for a while. I don't think she's through crying yet." Her face was white under the pinkish mustache left by the Popsicle. "I never saw anybody cry so hard, Rosie. I wonder if *my* mother would cry that much if she thought *you* were dead."

Rosie followed her friend downstairs. "I don't think it's just you she's crying about," she said slowly.

Angela looked disappointed. "Do you have any milk? Cookies? What else is she crying about?"

Rosie took the bottle of milk from the refrigerator while she thought about how to answer Angela's question. Lately Mama could be happy and then sad, cheerful and then glum, sometimes all in the same day. Up and down, up and down—it was like a roller-coaster ride, except that roller coasters were fun.

She shrugged. "Your mother's coming over," she said, to change the subject.

"Oh, no!" Angela dropped the cookies she was taking from the cookie jar. "Don't say anything about the Popsicle, okay?"

"She'll know," Rosie pointed out. "Look at your T-shirt."

Angela clutched her chest. "I'll wash it!" she exclaimed. She jumped up, glanced out the kitchen window, then hurried down the hall. "Tell her I'm in the bathroom, okay?"

Mrs. Carillo was one of Rosie's favorite people, and never more so than that afternoon. She marched in briskly, gave Rosie a hug, asked where Angela was, and then hurried upstairs. Rosie heard her say something outside the bathroom, and then Mama's bedroom door opened and closed. After that the house was silent except for the sound of water running in the bathroom.

Rosie went back to the porch and settled in Mama's rocking chair. She thought about all that had happened since the night the bat had hidden under the bed. That had been one of Mama's cheerful times; Rosie remembered how excited and pleased she'd been because she had chased the bat away without going next door for help.

Now she wondered if her mother would ever laugh again. She'd looked so sad and *lost*, lying on Rosie's bed.

Angela came out on the porch. The bright red stain on her T-shirt had changed to pale pink, and the shirt was very wet. "Where's my mom?" she asked nervously.

"Upstairs."

Angela slumped onto the couch. "I'm sorry I frightened your mother so much. I didn't wake up till she opened the wardrobe door, and I just sort of fell out. It scared me, too."

"You couldn't help it," Rosie said. "I'm sorry you were stuck in there for such a long time. I didn't know we were going to buy a new dress for the recital."

"The red one on the bed? It's pretty."

Rosie shrugged.

Angela pulled the wet T-shirt away from her skin.

"Rosie, do you think your mom is sick? I never saw anyone so—so sad before."

Rosie felt her eyes fill up with tears. Angela's question brought up a question of her own. If her mother was too sick or too sad to talk to her, and her father was too far away to help, what happened next?

Footsteps sounded in the upstairs hallway and on the stairs. Angela sank back against the wall and clutched a pillow across her chest, but Mrs. Carillo gave her only a glance as she came out on the porch.

"We'll talk when we get home, Miss Angela-the-Detective," she snapped. She pulled Papa's rocking chair close to Rosie and sat down. "Your mother's fine," she said. "She's going to nap for a little while, and then she'll be as good as new."

Rosie gripped the arms of the chair. "Are you sure?"

"Posi-lutely, abso-tively." Mrs. Carillo gave her arm a little pat. "See, your mom feels very bad because your father is so far away, Rosie. She misses him, same as you do, and she's scared, too. She got married when she was awfully young, and she's never been on her own before. She wants to show your father and you—and especially herself—that she can manage alone if she has to. And she was doing pretty well, I guess, till this burglar business started. It's upset her a lot, and today my darling daughter gave her the worst scare of all. That's why she was crying so hard. She's afraid she won't be able to cope while your dad is away."

Rosie bit her lip. "Will she cry again when she wakes up?"

"I don't think so. We had a good talk, and she promised to tell your father about the break-ins. She wanted to think she could handle the problem herself, but I hope I convinced her he has a right to know." She stood up and crooked a finger at Angela. "We're going home now—I left bread rising, and if I don't get back it's going to be all over the kitchen table. Would you like to come home with us for a while, Rosie?"

"Come!" Angela begged. But Rosie shrank back in the rocking chair.

"No, thanks," she said softly, "I guess I'll stay here."

Mrs. Carillo bent and kissed her on the cheek. "It's going to be all right, dear. Don't you worry. Promise?"

"I promise." Rosie waved good-bye to Angela, who looked as if she'd rather be going anywhere in the world than home, alone, with her mother. They crossed the yard and waved once more before disappearing through the row of lilac bushes.

Rosie had been alone in the house lots of times, but she had never felt as alone as she did now, with Mama asleep upstairs. She decided to stay where she was till her mother woke up. The sunny backyard seemed more inviting than the house.

She must have fallen asleep, because the telephone brought her to her feet with a gasp. For a moment she couldn't remember what had happened, and then the day's events came rushing back. Angela on the floor in front of the wardrobe. Before that, the piano lesson, with Mrs. Kramer and Mama feeling sorry for the poor girl with nine fingers. . . .

She went into the kitchen and lifted the phone. Her voice sounded strange—as if she had a cold.

"Rosie, is that you?"

"Papa!" Now she was wide awake.

"How's 'The Dance of the Dinosaurs' going? All set for Saturday?"

"Well—"

"I'll be there by noon or soon after, Rosie. My buddy's going to cover for me at the office, so I'll leave Milwaukee on the first bus in the morning."

"You mean you're coming to the recital?" Rosie clutched the phone so hard her hand ached.

"You bet I am. Where's your mother? I want to tell her, too."

"She's taking a nap," Rosie said. "Shall I wake her up?"

Her father said no, he would see them both on Saturday, and he could hardly wait. "We'll have a great weekend," he promised. "I can stay till the last bus Sunday evening. I don't care how late I get back here."

Now Rosie understood how Mama could be happy and sad at the same time. "What happens after Sunday?" she whispered.

A long wait for his answer. A long ride on the happy-sad roller coaster.

"I don't know exactly, kiddo." He sounded as if he were riding a roller coaster of his own. "We'll talk about it while I'm there—the three of us. We'll work things out, don't worry."

When Rosie put down the telephone, she thought about all the people who had told her not to worry today. Mrs. Kramer. Mama. Mrs. Carillo. Now Papa. When that many people said "Don't worry," it meant there was something to worry about.

Still, when she looked around the bright yellow kitchen, she discovered she felt better than she had five minutes ago. She wasn't really alone after all. Her father was coming home Saturday. Her mother was upstairs taking a nap. They would work out their problems together. *The three of us,* her father had promised.

Rosie went into the living room and gave each of the dinosaurs a pat. She loved the funny little pipe in the father's mouth, and the mother's wide straw hat. As soon as Mama woke up, she'd start working on that last page again. If her father was coming all the way from Milwaukee to hear her play, she supposed she'd have to try.

*At least,* she thought, *I'll look nice in the red dress.*

# CHAPTER 14

It was the day before the recital. When she was half awake, Rosie's stomach told her the Big Moment was very close. Butterflies fluttered inside her—or something much bigger than butterflies. Bats, maybe.

She slipped out of bed and tiptoed downstairs to the living room, where the dinosaur family waited on top of the piano. The early morning sun bathed them in gold. She narrowed her eyes, and the dinosaurs seemed to move in the shimmering light.

If she started practicing now, she'd wake up her mother, but she could review the memorizing. She sat in her father's armchair and, with her eyes closed, began to tell herself the story of "The Dance of the Dinosaurs." Line by line, page by page, she could see the notes as clearly as if she were looking at them.

From beginning to end—even the fast run on the last page—the notes were there in her head, waiting to be played. And she knew she could play them perfectly, except for that fast part. Her head knew them all. Her hands—her *hand*—did not.

"Hi, early bird." Mama stood in the doorway wrapped in her old blue bathrobe. She'd come downstairs so quietly that Rosie hadn't heard her. She looked pale and tired, but at least she was smiling. Maybe it was because Papa was coming home for the weekend.

"What are you doing, sitting here all by your lonesome?"

"Practicing," Rosie explained, "in my head."

Mama nodded. "Something nice happened after you went to bed last night. Angela's mother called and invited us to their house for supper tonight. Won't that be fun?"

Rosie decided she *loved* Mrs. Carillo. Angela's mother must have guessed that they needed some cheering up.

After breakfast Rosie went back to the piano, but she still couldn't get through the last page without stopping. If the dinosaurs plodded ever so slowly up and down the mountain instead of dancing, then she could play all the notes. But as soon as she speeded up, her fingers stumbled over each other. Rosie imagined the dinosaur family looking down at her with disgust from the top of the piano.

It was the dreariest morning she could remember.

When she was through practicing, she tried to read a mystery, but she couldn't sit still. She called Angela twice. The first time she learned that her friend had lost her allowance for two weeks because she'd played detective in Rosie's house. The second time, Angela told her that Mary Jean was coming for supper, too. Rosie was sorry to hear that. She wasn't ready to face Mary Jean again . . . especially on the night before the recital.

At noon, Mama made sandwiches and they ate on the back porch. Afterward, Rosie held the ladder while her mother climbed up to see if the eave troughs needed cleaning. Each time she looked at the clock, only five minutes had passed.

"You might practice some more, hon," Mama suggested toward the end of the afternoon.

Rosie shook her head. What was the use? If she practiced all night, it wouldn't make any difference. Her right hand couldn't do what she wanted it to do.

She was relieved when five o'clock finally came and they could go to Angela's house.

"Let's walk," Rosie suggested. "We can cut through backyards, same as Angela and I do."

Mama took the car keys from the nail in the back hall. "Not a chance," she said. "It'll be dark by the time we come home. There was a time when I enjoyed a walk on a summer night, but not now." Rosie knew she was thinking about the dark figure in the backyard.

When they drove up the steep hill to the Carillos'

house, Angela and Mary Jean were waiting on the front steps.

"So that's Mary Jean," Mama said, as if she'd been wondering what the star of the recital would look like. "She's pretty—but what's the matter with Angela?"

Rosie saw that Angela's mouth was set in a glum line.

"Oh, dear," Mama said as they climbed out of the car, "I hope she isn't being punished for what happened yesterday. I shouldn't have gotten so upset. . . ."

"No allowance for two weeks," Rosie whispered. "But she was okay when I talked to her this morning."

They went up the walk, and Mrs. Carpenter continued on into the house after saying hello to the girls. Rosie settled on the top step and waited for someone to tell her what was wrong.

Mary Jean finally broke the silence. "Angela's father lost his job today," she said solemnly. "If he doesn't get another one, they might have to move out of their house."

Rosie gasped. "No, he didn't," she said. But why would anyone lie about a thing like that?

"Yes, he did," Angela said. "The Athena mine is closing, and so he got laid off. And if you get laid off, you can't pay for your house and pretty soon you have to move out. I hate it! My dad's been sitting at the kitchen table ever since he came home. He just keeps drinking coffee and doing this—" She tap-tapped on the step with her fingertips. "And just when I got my wallpaper," she added mournfully.

"Oh, Angela." Last month, as a birthday surprise, Mr. Carillo had covered Angela's bedroom walls with yellow roses. Her mother had dyed some sheets yellow to make a bedspread and draperies, and now, on even the dreariest day, the room looked as if it were full of sunshine.

"Maybe you won't have to move," Mary Jean said. "Maybe Uncle Frank will get another job right away." She patted her cousin's hand, but Angela pulled away.

"There aren't any other jobs," Angela said. "All the mines are closing, and that's what my dad does. He's a miner. You don't understand. You don't know how lucky you are." She was answering Mary Jean, but she glared at Rosie, too. They were both lucky, her look said. Their fathers had jobs.

Rosie shifted on the step. She hadn't thought of herself as lucky that her father had a job—any job. She'd only thought about how terrible it was to have him working in another city.

Mrs. Carillo opened the screen door behind them. "Hi, Rosie. Come on inside, girls. Time to eat. I hope you're ready for spaghetti and meatballs."

Rosie heard Mrs. Carillo whisper, "Cheer up, honey," as Angela passed her on the way into the house.

It wasn't the kind of supper hour that Rosie remembered from other evenings with the Carillos. Angela's father usually had a supply of riddles for the girls, but tonight he just smiled whenever anyone looked at him and didn't seem to hear what was being said. Mrs. Carillo and Mama did most of the talking. They discussed recipes and the recital and the cupboards Mama had painted.

"Your kitchen looks nice," Mrs. Carillo said. "And of course Angela thinks it's great because yellow is her favorite color." She pressed her lips together as soon as the words were out, as if she were sorry she'd said them.

Angela sighed. Rosie knew she was thinking about her yellow bedroom.

It was a relief to go back to the front porch after the last of the spumoni ice cream had been eaten and the dishes had been carried to the kitchen.

"What do you want to do?" Angela asked. She sounded as if *she* didn't want to do anything but sit on the steps and stare into the twilight.

"We could roller-skate," Rosie suggested. "I put mine in the trunk of the car—just in case."

"Roller-skate!" Mary Jean repeated. "Where?"

Angela's frown started to fade. She waved her arm at the steep hill in front of them. "It's terrific, Mary Jean," she said, beginning to sound like her enthusiastic self again. "Rosie and I race all the time." She jumped up. "I got new skates for my birthday, but you can use my old ones. Your feet might be a *little* smaller but—"

"No way," Mary Jean said. "I hate hills."

"Then you can be the judge and decide who's the fastest," Angela said. "I'll get my skates."

Mary Jean looked annoyed, but Angela was already on her way into the house. When she returned, she and Rosie put on their skates quickly.

"You first," Rosie said. It was good to see her friend smiling again.

"She's going the wrong way," Mary Jean said, as Angela set off for the top of the hill.

"We always start up there," Rosie explained. "By the time we get this far, we're practically flying."

Angela reached the top of the hill and waved to them. Then she started down, using short strokes at first, to pick up speed, then longer ones. When she passed Rosie and Mary Jean, she coasted and waved, her face glowing.

Mary Jean shuddered. "I'd never do that," she said. "What if she fell—"

"She never falls," Rosie said. "Neither do I. Just watch me."

"What about your hands? I mean—" She stopped, and Rosie knew she was sorry she'd mentioned hands.

"What do you mean?"

"All I meant was, you might fall and hurt yourself. Then you couldn't play in the recital tomorrow."

"I never fall."

Rosie started up the hill. *You might fall and hurt your hands*. That could happen. And if it did, she wouldn't have to play in the recital.

It was always a surprise to discover how steep the

hill was when she reached the top and looked down. Rosie took a deep breath. She waved at Mary Jean, and at Angela who was starting back up from the bottom.

Six or eight little steps and she was off, her legs stretching into long, gliding strokes. Houses flashed by, blurring into a single house. As she passed Angela's front steps, she darted a glance over her shoulder and saw Mary Jean watching in amazement.

*You could fall.*

She swooshed past Angela, and then, too soon, she was at the bottom of the hill. She coasted to a stop and turned at the curb with a flourish.

Angela waited for her to catch up, so they could climb the rest of the way together. "Roller-skating's more fun than anything," she said. "Oh, Rosie, what if we move to a place where there aren't any hills?"

"You won't." Rosie tried to sound sure. "There are hills just about everywhere. Besides, you don't know for sure that you're going to move."

When they reached the Carillos' house, Mary Jean looked at them with something close to awe. "I never saw anybody skate that fast," she said.

"Let's do it again," Angela said. "We'll race this time." She was already starting up the hill.

Usually when they raced, Rosie won. Her legs were longer. This time she moved ahead before they were halfway down the hill. *I could fall.* The thought was back, following her down the hill like a pesky bee. *I wouldn't have to do it on purpose. I could just close my eyes, hit a bumpy spot* . . . It would hurt, but nothing could be as bad as the recital was going to be.

"Look out—I'm going to pass you." Angela was at her shoulder, her face bright red with strain.

"No, you're not," Rosie shouted. She lengthened her strides and pulled ahead again. It was no use thinking about falling. She wanted to win. She wanted to win more than she wanted to fall.

Still, when they reached the bottom, breathless and giggling and Rosie saw her mother come out on the Carillos' porch, she was almost sorry there wasn't time for another race. Falling had been her last chance to escape the recital. Now there was no way out.

They took Mary Jean home and then headed back across town to the old gray house. Mama had left some lights burning, and the house looked warm and welcoming in the dark.

"I'll miss it terribly if we have to leave it," Mama said softly. It was the first time she'd spoken on the way home, and the first time she'd ever admitted they might have to leave their house.

"I felt sorry for the Carillos tonight," she went on. "It made me think. Just last night Angela's mother was being so kind, trying to make me feel better— and now she has this terrible worry. Your father didn't lose his job in Dexter, you know—he was promoted to a better job when he moved. So many people have lost their jobs since the mines started closing, but he was promoted. I guess we should be thankful."

"I guess," Rosie agreed. She was thankful just to

see her mother smiling again, even though it was a sad little smile.

"So!" Mama said suddenly. "Tomorrow's the recital, isn't it? At last." She was pretending that the recital hardly mattered, that she'd forgotten how close it was.

"Daddy's coming home," Rosie said. "That's more important."

"The most important thing in the world," Mama agreed. She began singing the words—*Coming home, coming home*—and Rosie sang them with her. She kept them in her mind—the most important thing—all the time she was getting ready for bed, and afterward, lying very still in the moonlight.

*Coming home.* The words were like a prayer that could keep away bad thoughts. They echoed in her head, so at first she didn't hear the movement inside the wardrobe.

# CHAPTER 15

It was a soft, scuffling sound that reminded Rosie of the night there had been a bat under her bed on the porch. But this wasn't a bat. Something big was making the hangers clink against each other. Something big—she shrank against the wall, the bed sheet drawn up to her chin—something big was opening the wardrobe doors.

The front of the wardrobe was silvery in the moonlight, with a black line down the middle that widened as the doors parted. Rosie screamed. Her nightmare was actually happening—the one she'd had right after the wardrobe was delivered. In a moment she would see the old man's face peering out at her.

She screamed again, and now she could hear Mama running up the stairs. It seemed forever before she reached the bedroom doorway, and when she did, Rosie couldn't look at her. She didn't dare take her eyes away from the wardrobe.

"Honey, what's wrong?" Her mother switched on the light.

Rosie pointed at the partly opened doors. "In there," she squeaked, "somebody's in there."

"Oh, Rosie, no." Mama stopped as the hangers clattered together. Then she hurtled across the bedroom and threw herself against the wardrobe doors. With the doors shut tight, it sounded as if an earthquake were trapped inside the wardrobe.

"Rosie, quick!" Mama gritted the words through clenched teeth. "Call the police. No, run next door and get Mr. Larsen. Hurry!"

Rosie was too frightened to move. The wardrobe was teetering now, threatening to fall. Mama braced herself, leaning hard against the doors, trying not to slip on the rag rug bunched up in the middle of the floor.

"Rosie, for heaven's sake, hurry. I can't do this much longer. Get Mr. Larsen!"

Rosie slid from under the sheet and stumbled backward to the door. This nightmare was worse than the first one, because she couldn't wake up. If she turned away from the wardrobe for even a second, the burglar—the dark figure she'd seen in the backyard—would burst out and attack her mother. If she went next door for Mr. Larsen, she'd come back and find Mama on the floor the way they'd found Angela, only

this time the blood would be real and Mama would
be—

"ROSIE! WILL YOU GO!"

She was halfway down the hall when there was a
crash from the bedroom. A wail rose above the
thunder of wood on wood and ended abruptly.

She dashed back to the bedroom. The wardrobe lay
on its side, one door closed, the other hanging open.
A thin arm and a grubby hand extended from the open
door. Mama stood in front of the fallen wardrobe,
peering down at the arm.

Rosie stepped backward. "I'll get Mr. Larsen," she
said. But now her mother leaned over to open the
other door. When she turned the knob, the burglar
rolled out and huddled on the floor.

"This wardrobe produces a new body every day,"
Mama said. "And they're all under the age of twelve."

"I'm twelve and a half," the burglar said. He sat up
and touched a purplish lump on his forehead. "It
hurts!"

"I should think it would," Mama said. She
crouched to get a better look. "Rosie, run downstairs
and wrap some ice cubes in a towel. This bump's
getting bigger by the minute." When Rosie hesitated,
she snapped her fingers. "Wake up and go, hon.
There's nothing to be afraid of now."

Rosie ran downstairs to the kitchen, found a soft
linen towel, and dropped a half-dozen ice cubes on it.
Then she gathered up the edges to make a bag and
hurried back upstairs.

The burglar-boy had moved to Rosie's bed, and Mama stood in front of him, her hands on her hips. She took the ice bag and pressed it on the boy's forehead, holding it firmly when he tried to push her hand away.

Rosie peered over her mother's shoulder. "I think I've seen him before," she said uncertainly. "Or else I've seen somebody who looks like him." Big ears, lots of freckles, thick, sand-colored eyebrows. . . . She remembered a gruff voice saying, "Hey, kid, what happened to your hand?"

"What's your name?" Mama asked the boy.

He glared up at them. With one eye covered by the ice bag, he looked like a pirate.

"I said, what's your name?" Mama glared back. "You can tell me, or you can tell the police. If you don't speak up, you can bet I'm going to call the police and tell them we caught you hiding in our wardrobe, getting ready to do heaven knows what."

"Not getting ready to do anything," the boy muttered. "I already done it. I was lookin' for something."

"Looking for what? In *our* house?"

Rosie tugged at the sleeve of Mama's robe. "What was the name of the man who brought the wardrobe here?" she whispered.

Mama shook her head impatiently. "I don't see—" she began, and then she stared at the burglar-boy. "You're right, Rosie, he's the image of the man who sold the wardrobe to me. His name was—let me see

—it was Carver. Is that your name, young man?"

He nodded sullenly. "Marty Carver."

"Well, why didn't you say so, Marty Carver?" Mama demanded. "And are you the person who's been sneaking into our house every time our backs are turned?"

"And standing out in the backyard in the dark?" Rosie added. "I saw you there."

The boy made a face and pushed the ice bag away from his eye. "I only come all the way in one other time," he protested. "I come in the back porch a couple times when I thought nobody was home, and I come upstairs to look through the wardrobe once before. Just once." He moved the ice bag again, and winced. "I bet I'm going to die," he said fearfully. "I think I broke somethin' in my head."

"I doubt that," Mama said. "You're banged up a little, but you'll live." The quiver was gone from her voice. She sat down on one end of the bed and motioned Rosie to the chair in front of the desk.

"Now, Marty Carver," she said, "I want you to tell us exactly why you've been doing these terrible things. If you don't, I'm going to call the police first and your father second, and we'll let them get the whole story out of you."

The boy sat up, moving carefully and holding the ice bag in place. "I was just tryin' to get what belongs to us," he said. "What belongs to my pa. I thought they was in there." He pointed to the wardrobe lying on its side. "But they ain't. I looked."

"Looked for what? Speak up."

"The bankbooks," Marty mumbled. "A whole bunch of 'em, maybe. They was my grandpa's, and I thought he might have hid 'em in the wardrobe a long time ago."

Mama looked astonished. "Now, why would he do a thing like that? Bankbooks belong in a strongbox. And wouldn't your father know if they were there? That wardrobe was shined up as nice as can be when I bought it. There certainly weren't any bankbooks lying around in it."

Marty Carver sighed. "No, ma'am, I see that now. Been through the thing twice. I was just goin' to go home when I heard you drive in the garage. There wasn't time to run, so I climbed inside the wardrobe. I was goin' to wait till you was asleep and then sneak out."

"But why didn't your father just call and say he wanted to look for the bankbooks?" Mama demanded. "He certainly would have been welcome."

"He said from the beginning they couldn't be in there. It was just me thinkin' they might be. See, my grandpa liked his secrets—never told anybody what he had. He was real nice, but he liked his secrets. After he died, Mr. Graf—that's my grandpa's friend—he told Pa that Grandpa had money in lots of different banks under different, made-up names. Grandpa told Mr. Graf he was going to hide the bankbooks in a really safe place."

"But why?" Mama asked again. "Surely he wanted your folks to have his money when he was gone."

Marty took the ice bag away from his forehead and looked from Mama to Rosie, a pleading kind of look. "He was real nice," he repeated. "But when he got old, he got kind of mixed up. Maybe by then he even forgot he had money in those banks. Or maybe he thought my pa would be able to find the books when the time came. Or maybe—"

"Or maybe he got old and sick and just thought up that whole story because it made him feel good," Mama said softly. "Did Mr. Graf ever *see* those bankbooks?"

Marty shook his head.

"So *you* decided he might have hidden the bankbooks in the wardrobe . . .?"

"It was his wardrobe," Marty said. "It was in his bedroom. I thought that's where he'd put them."

"If he ever had them," Mama said. "If."

"He had 'em," Marty said stubbornly, "I know it. And now my pa's out of work and he needs money, and it's probably just sitting in some banks somewhere, and we don't know where. So I had to look, didn't I?"

Mama sighed. "I suppose you did," she said, "but I do wish you'd just knocked on the door and explained the whole thing instead of sneaking in and scaring us half to death. And by the way, how did you get in here this time? I had the house locked up tight."

"Ladder," Marty mumbled. "You left it up against the porch. The window was unlocked, so I just come on through."

Rosie slid to the floor and peered into the wardrobe. Her clothes had tumbled off their hangers and were lying in a heap.

"Don't bother lookin'," Marty said. He put the ice bag on his head again. "They ain't there. I've looked everywhere. I thought there might be a secret compartment. My grandpa was a carpenter, so he could build one if he wanted to. My pa said that was a crazy idea, but I say it could have been that way."

"Well." Mama patted Marty Carver's knee and stood up. "If you feel well enough to help, we'll stand the wardrobe up the way it's supposed to be, and then we'll give it one more going-over together. So you'll be satisfied."

"No use," Marty said. "But I'll help you put it back up. It's my fault if it's broke."

"That's true," Mama agreed. "You come up to the top end with me. Rosie, you go to the bottom and sort of guide it into place when we lift."

Rosie edged around the wardrobe. "We should fix the bottom before we stand it up," she suggested. "It looks like it's going to fall apart when we move it."

"Not this wardrobe," Mama said sharply. "It's solid oak." She bent down and looked inside. "The floor is perfectly okay." Then she stepped around the wardrobe and stood next to Rosie.

"My, oh, my," she said, after a minute. "Rosie

you're a smart girl. Somebody has fitted a sheet of plywood over the outside bottom. It's thin as cardboard and starting to shatter."

"Hey!" The ice bag dropped to the floor.

"We'll need a hammer to rip off the rest of it," Mama said. "Rosie—"

Rosie raced downstairs, two steps at a time. Wait till she told Angela about this! She found the hammer on the tool rack in the basement and dashed back up the stairs to see what would happen next.

Marty snatched the hammer from her hand and began whacking the plywood bottom with all his might.

"Don't wreck the wardrobe, for goodness' sake," Mama protested. "Just slide the prongs into one of the cracks and pull."

He did as he was told, his face red with excitement. A section of the board broke loose with a loud *crack*.

"There's nothing there," Rosie said. "Just more wood. The real bottom."

"Tear off the rest of the plywood, Marty," Mama said, "and please be careful."

The boy forced the prongs of the hammer under the remaining strip of plywood and pulled. At first the wood held firm. Then it gave way, so suddenly that Marty rocked back on his heels. When he regained his balance, a long brown envelope lay on the floor at his feet.

"Oh, my," Mama murmured, "oh, my, oh, my, oh, my." She sounded as if she were praying.

Marty tore open the envelope and shook out the contents. Four little booklets lay on the floor.

"I don't believe it," Mama said. "I just don't. They really are bankbooks."

"I'm going to call Angela," Rosie said, but she didn't move. Marty was opening one of the books.

"Warren Olds," he read, squinting at the first page. "That's a made-up name, for sure; but it's my grandpa's handwriting. His first name was Warren, and his ma's last name was Olds before she got married." He turned a page and whistled. "Four thousand dollars," he said, and his voice shook.

Mama picked up another book and handed it to him.

"Jessie Olds," he read. "Jessie is my mom's name. There's thirty-nine hundred and twelve dollars in this one."

The third book carried his grandpa's own name— Warren Carver—and was from a bank in Madison, Wisconsin. "Three thousand dollars and eighty-seven cents. He used to go to Madison every once in a while to see a doctor."

He opened the last book, and this time he didn't say anything at all. Rosie could tell he was trying not to cry. "Look," he said finally, and he held out the book to Mama and then to Rosie. The name on the first page was Martin Carver. The bank was in Michigan.

"He saved up two thousand dollars and put my name on the book," Marty said. He wiped his eyes with the back of his hand. "Caught a cold," he muttered.

Mama scooped up the bankbooks and put them back into the envelope. "That's what happens to boys who stand around in the dark waiting to break into somebody's house," she said.

But she was smiling when she said it.

# CHAPTER 16

"Wait'll I tell Angela," Rosie said. "She won't believe what's happened."

"Wait'll we tell your father," Mama replied. "He won't believe it either."

Rosie sat at the kitchen table, watching her mother make cocoa. Mama's face shone with excitement, and she seemed to glide around the kitchen, graceful as a ballet dancer in her old blue bathrobe and floppy slippers.

"Actually, I can't believe it either," Mama said. "When I saw that wardrobe door opening, all I wanted to do was grab your hand and run out of the house. That would have been the *sensible* thing to do. I can't believe I stayed there and held that door shut. If it had been a real burglar inside . . ." She shuddered. "Don't you ever do anything that foolish, Rosie."

Rosie nodded, but she knew Mama was glad they hadn't run.

"That boy didn't even say thank you before he went home," Rosie said. "He should have said thank you. He never would have found the bankbooks if we hadn't helped him look."

Mama put a plate of gingersnap cookies on the table. "The look on his face was thank-you enough for me," she said. "Did you notice his pants, Rosie? Patches on both knees and a mend in the seat! The money in those bankbooks is going to be very welcome. We'll call his father tomorrow if they don't call us first."

Tomorrow. Rosie looked at the clock and put down her half-eaten cookie. It was almost ten o'clock. For a little while she'd forgotten all about tomorrow. But now Saturday was just two hours away. The recital was like a train chugging down the track right toward her. She couldn't get out of its way.

"Drink your cocoa and let's go to bed," Mama said. "Tomorrow's going to be a big day. A wonderful day. Your father will be sitting here in this kitchen. Think of that!"

Rosie rinsed her cocoa mug and went slowly up the stairs, trying to pretend that the only important thing about Saturday was that Papa would be home again. *It's going to be a double-terrific day,* she told herself.

But she didn't believe it, not for a minute. Papa would come home, and then they would have to go to the recital, and "The Dance of the Dinosaurs" would spoil everything.

# CHAPTER 17

He wasn't quite as tall as Rosie remembered him, but he insisted he hadn't shrunk. He said he looked shorter to Rosie because she had grown at least an inch this summer. Anyway, an hour after they picked him up at the bus station, it seemed as if he'd never been away at all. Mama must have felt the same way, because Rosie had to remind her to show him the yellow cupboards.

"Beautiful," Papa said. "Somebody around here is a first-class painter."

Mama looked pleased. "Oh, well, the kitchen needed a little color," she said, as if all that work had been nothing at all. "And it'll make a good impression if we have to sell."

He hugged Mama with one arm and Rosie with the

other. "My girls," he said, the way he'd said it about a thousand times before.

Lunch was special—shrimp salad with hard-boiled eggs, homemade muffins, and Papa's favorite chocolate cake with fudge frosting. While they ate, Rosie and her mother took turns telling about the burglar.

"Then there really was someone in the house that day we were talking on the phone and you sounded so scared," Papa said, looking sort of scared, himself.

"There really was, and last night we caught him," Rosie said. "Mama and I." She described how they had seen the wardrobe door opening, and how Mama had tried to keep the burglar inside while Rosie ran for help.

"Only the wardrobe fell over and Marty Carver fell out and the bankbooks he was looking for were hidden in the bottom," she finished with a rush. "And now the Carvers are rich."

"Not rich," Mama said gently, "but they can stop worrying about money for a while. I talked to Mr. Carver this morning, and he's very grateful—to Marty and to us."

Papa shook his head. "All I can think of is how you two might have been in real danger," he said, "and I wasn't here to help."

Mama cut another slice of cake and put it on his plate. "We managed," she said proudly, "but we're certainly glad you're here now."

"Not half as glad as I am," Papa said. He started on

the second piece of cake, then glanced at his watch. "What time is the recital?" he asked. "Do I have to hurry through this, or can I take my time?"

Rosie slumped in her chair.

"We have an hour," Mama said. "You can take as long as you want, while Rosie and I get beautiful. Rosie has a new dress for the recital."

"It's red," Rosie said, because now they were both looking at her.

"Red's my favorite color," her father said. "As if you didn't know." All of a sudden his voice was phony-cheerful, the way Mama's had been when they were shopping for the red dress. Rosie wondered if he had guessed how scared she was.

Later, when they were dressed and ready to go, Rosie decided he did know. He was in the living room looking at the dinosaurs lined up on the piano, when she came downstairs.

"Great dress, kiddo," he said. "You look ready for anything."

*Huh!* Rosie thought. *Ready for nothing.*

"The dinosaurs look nice there," Papa said. "When I was packing them up to send to you, I thought, 'Rosie will put them on top of the piano.' And you did. Why do I always know what you're going to do?"

She couldn't smile. Her hands were clammy, and her stomach was churning. She didn't want to be standing here in her new red dress, waiting to play in the recital. She wanted to run back upstairs to her bedroom. Hide under the covers with Bert Bear. Or maybe hide in the wardrobe, the way Marty Carver had, with the doors closed tight.

"I think I'm going to throw up," she said.

"No, you're not. You're nervous about playing and that can make the old stomach feel peculiar. It's nothing to worry about. You look beautiful in your new dress, and you're going to do just fine."

*Fine!* Rosie thought. *Fine!*

"The dinosaurs tell me you're worried about the last part of your piece," Papa went on. "The part that's supposed to go fast."

"It was Mama who told you," Rosie said in a small voice. "The dinosaurs don't talk."

"Well, whoever. The point is, you don't have to worry, kiddo. You do the very best you can, and it'll be okay. If you have to stop ten times, it'll still be okay, as long as you're doing your best."

Rosie closed her eyes. She could taste the shrimp salad. "We'd better go," she said faintly. "It's getting late."

Mrs. Kramer's living room was full of folding chairs arranged in rows with an aisle down the middle. Most of the chairs were already filled with mothers and fathers and aunts and uncles and grandparents. Mrs. Kramer motioned to Rosie to come to the front where the students were to sit.

"You'll do fine," Papa whispered and gave her another hug.

Mama hugged her, too. "Just fine," she said.

Rosie wished they'd stop saying that word. She'd never feel fine again. For the rest of her life, when people said, "How are you?" she'd have to answer, *"Terrible!"*

Mary Jean was already sitting in the front row. She patted the chair next to her, and Rosie sat down.

"I saved it for you," Mary Jean whispered. "Want to hear something disgusting? My brother is here."

Rosie looked around nervously. "Where?"

"In the car. My mother and father are staying outside with him till the last minute. They didn't want to bring him at all, but he kicked the baby-sitter in the knee, and she went home." Mary Jean clenched her fists. "I'll kill him if he makes a noise while I'm playing."

Rosie stared at the grand piano, just a few feet away. She'd always thought it was beautiful, but today it looked like a big, hulking monster.

Mrs. Kramer, standing next to the piano, looked different, too. Her hair was piled on top of her head like a mushroom cap, and her dress was a funny pea-soup color. "We're ready to begin," she warned, and waited for the whispering to stop.

"Don't *want* to sit down," a small voice said from the back of the room.

"There he is," Mary Jean groaned. "What did I tell you!"

Mrs. Kramer pretended not to hear. She nodded at a little girl at the end of the row, and the recital began.

The youngest players came first. Rosie listened numbly, as they sat down at the monster-piano, one after the other, and played short pieces from the first-year book. She had played some of these songs herself, two years ago, but they sounded babyish now. "The Dance of the Dinosaurs" was much, much harder.

*Too hard,* she thought desperately. *Too hard for nine fingers.* She folded the skirt of her new dress over her right hand and wished she were anywhere else but here. Racing downhill with Angela. Picnicking on the raft. Anywhere in the whole world but here.

"Wanna go *home!*"

Eldon's voice rose above the clapping, as a boy in a white shirt and blue trousers bowed and hurried back to his seat. Mary Jean put her hands over her ears.

Rosie longed to turn around to see where her father and mother were sitting. She needed to look at them. But if she turned, everyone would see how frightened she was. They'd laugh or—worse—they'd feel sorry for her even before she played.

The music became more difficult.

Rosie glanced at the pale blue program Mrs. Kramer had given her as they came in. There was one more name on the list, and then it would be her turn.

Jennifer Wiley was Rosie's age but hadn't been taking lessons as long. She walked to the piano and sat down as calmly as if she were at home in her living room, playing for no one but herself. Her piece was called "The Zookeeper's March." Rosie tried to imagine the animals in the zoo marching along, two by two, but all she could think of was that Jennifer was a good player. She wasn't making a single mistake. None of the players had stumbled, or started over, or hit a sour note, so far. Rosie Carpenter would be the first.

"Wanna go *now!*" It was Eldon again, his voice rising shrilly just as Jennifer finished playing. There was a thud, then applause.

"He's kicking," Mary Jean whispered. "He's going to spoil my piece—I just know it." She glanced down at the program. "Hey, you're next," she said, as if she'd just remembered Rosie was to perform, too.

Rosie stood up. She remembered a time when she was little, and she'd climbed the ladder of the tallest slide in the park. Someone had told her only babies used the smaller ones. When she looked down from the top, the slide had seemed unbelievably long and steep. She had the same feeling now that she'd had then. Once she started, there would be no turning back. She would be all alone, and no one could help her.

"Go *on!*" Mary Jean whispered impatiently.

Rosie slid onto the piano bench, keeping her back straight and her head up the way Mrs. Kramer had taught her. She wasn't supposed to look at the audience, but she couldn't resist a quick glance. Halfway down the aisle her parents sat, smiling at her. Smiling, but looking worried, too, Rosie thought. She tried to smile back, but her lips wouldn't move. Papa made a thumbs-up gesture, and at that moment Eldon the Horrible appeared at the end of the aisle. He stood there for a moment, then dropped to his knees and scrambled away from his mother's outstretched arms.

Rosie began to play. The father dinosaur clump-clumped around the valley. He bellowed with anger because he couldn't find food for his family. Then his roars faded, and the mother and daughter dinosaurs watched sadly as he clumped away from them to hunt somewhere else.

Out of the corner of her eye, Rosie saw movement. Eldon was crawling up the aisle. As he passed each row, he kicked the nearest chair, then scuttled a little farther. A father reached for him and missed.

Rosie looked away. The mother and daughter dinosaurs wandered around together, waiting for the father to come home . . . a sad, lonely little melody. She made herself think about how bad they must feel. Made herself ignore an especially loud *thunk* as Eldon crashed into someone's ankles. "Stop him!" a voice hissed. But he kept on coming.

Rosie played, and now Eldon was close to the front row. He was making clucking noises that were not quite drowned out by the music until the storm began in the dinosaurs' valley. Rosie took a deep breath and hit the big thunder chords that were fun to play. *Think about the poor dinosaurs in the cave,* she ordered herself. *Think about the storm. Don't think about Eldon who is . . .*

UNDER THE PIANO!

Afterward, Rosie could remember playing the part where the storm ended. What was Eldon doing under there? The father dinosaur returned to his valley, and his family ran to meet him, so happy, their huge dinosaur-feet barely touched the ground. Something brushed Rosie's ankle, just as the dinosaurs began their run to the top of the mountain. Eldon somersaulted out from under the piano. Head down, puffing noisily, he balanced himself against the end of the piano bench and tried to stand on his head.

Rosie heard the audience gasp, but she didn't stop playing. Better to have him in sight than to wonder what was happening under the piano. Her fingers raced to the top of the mountain without hesitating, then down, down, down, without missing a note. She didn't have time to wonder whether she could do it. She was too busy wondering if Eldon would tumble over backward and land on the piano keys.

"The Dance of the Dinosaurs" and the headstand ended at almost the same moment. As Rosie played the final chord, Eldon tumbled in a heap beside the bench. She stood up, stepped carefully around him, and curtsied the way Mrs. Kramer had showed her.

There was a small commotion in the back of the room, and Mrs. Weiss dashed up the aisle. She grabbed Eldon and dragged him away, through the arch in the back of the living room and out the front door. For a moment the little boy's furious screams were the only sound breaking the sunny afternoon stillness. Then the audience began to clap. They clapped and clapped. Eldon's father even stood up and clapped over his head so Rosie would be sure to see him. Mrs. Kramer clapped. The piano students clapped, too, except for Mary Jean. Rosie saw her mother and father smiling proudly.

When the clapping finally stopped, Mary Jean went to the piano. She played well, and the audience clapped loudly for her, too, but not as loudly or as long as they had for Rosie. After all, she hadn't had to perform while Eldon tumbled around being horrible.

Rosie looked down at her hands in wonder. Nine good fingers had known what to do after all. Her father had been right. Maybe, she thought, still hardly able to believe it was all over, maybe there could be more than one star in this recital.

Mrs. Kramer stood next to the piano and invited everyone to come into the dining room for punch and cookies. Rosie saw Mama and Papa waiting for her, but she could only wave at them. People were crowding around her, telling her how well she played.

"I don't see how you did it," a lady said. "That dreadful child . . .."

When Rosie finally reached her mother and father, they took turns hugging her. "You were great!" Papa said. "Terrific! I wanted to strangle that little monster, but you didn't let him bother you a bit. We're proud of you, honey."

Rosie floated into the dining room. That was how she felt—as if her feet weren't touching the ground. The recital was over, and she had played well.

"I could eat twenty cookies," she said.

Mama giggled. "You've earned them," she whispered.

"Rose, dear, Eldon has something to say to you."

Rosie whirled around and saw Mrs. Weiss behind her. She had her hands on Eldon's shoulders. The little boy's face was blotchy, and his eyes were puffed from crying. Mrs. Weiss must have scolded him hard. Rosie wondered if he'd ever been scolded before.

"Go ahead, Eldon." Mrs. Weiss gave him a shake.

"I'm sorry," Eldon mumbled. He looked ready to cry again.

Rosie couldn't stand it. She wanted everybody to be as happy as she was. She tried to think of something to make Eldon feel better.

"It's okay," she said. "Want to see a magic trick?"

Eldon nodded. She held out her right hand. "Count my fingers," she said.

Eldon counted, "One, two, three, four." He counted again. He looked at his own hand, then back at hers. "How do you do that?" he demanded.

"It's a secret." Rosie laughed, and after a moment Eldon laughed, too.

Rosie looked up and saw her mother and father watching her. "I feel so good," Rosie said. "I want to feel like this forever and ever."

"I do, too," Mama said.

"So do I," Papa agreed. "Three happy dinosaurs, that's us. Come on, Rosie. You'd better get started on those twenty cookies."

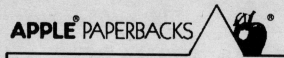

# APPLE® PAPERBACKS

## *Pick an Apple and Polish Off Some Great Reading!*

### BEST-SELLING APPLE TITLES

☐ MT43944-8 **Afternoon of the Elves** Janet Taylor Lisle — $2.75

☐ MT43109-9 **Boys Are Yucko** Anna Grossnickle Hines — $2.75

☐ MT43473-X **The Broccoli Tapes** Jan Slepian — $2.95

☐ MT42709-1 **Christina's Ghost** Betty Ren Wright — $2.75

☐ MT43461-6 **The Dollhouse Murders** Betty Ren Wright — $2.75

☐ MT43444-6 **Ghosts Beneath Our Feet** Betty Ren Wright — $2.75

☐ MT44351-8 **Help! I'm a Prisoner in the Library** Eth Clifford — $2.75

☐ MT44567-7 **Leah's Song** Eth Clifford — $2.75

☐ MT43618-X **Me and Katie (The Pest)** Ann M. Martin — $2.75

☐ MT41529-8 **My Sister, The Creep** Candice F. Ransom — $2.75

☐ MT42883-7 **Sixth Grade Can Really Kill You** Barthe DeClements — $2.75

☐ MT40409-1 **Sixth Grade Secrets** Louis Sachar — $2.75

☐ MT42882-9 **Sixth Grade Sleepover** Eve Bunting — $2.75

☐ MT41732-0 **Too Many Murphys** Colleen O'Shaughnessy McKenna — $2.75

---

*Available wherever you buy books, or use this order form.*

**Scholastic Inc., P.O. Box 7502, 2931 East McCarty Street, Jefferson City, MO 65102**

Please send me the books I have checked above. I am enclosing $_____ (please add $2.00 to cover shipping and handling). Send check or money order — no cash or C.O.D.s please.

Name _____

Address _____

City_____ State/Zip _____

Please allow four to six weeks for delivery. Offer good in the U.S.A. only. Sorry, mail orders are not available to residents of Canada. Prices subject to change.

APP591